27/6/ 17

EssexWorks.
For a better quality of life

CoL

Please return this book on or before the date shown above. To renew go to www.essex.gov.uk/libraries, ring 0845 603 7628 or go to any Essex library.

Essex County Council

WOUNDS

Maureen Duffy is a British poet, playwright and novelist. After a tough childhood, Duffy took her degree in English from King's College London. She turned to writing full-time as a poet and playwright after being commissioned to produce a screenplay by Granada Television. Her first novel, *That's How It Was* (1962), was published to great acclaim. Her first openly lesbian novel was *The Microcosm* (1966), set in the famous Gateways club in London. Her *Collected Poems, 1949-84* appeared in 1985. Maureen's most recent poetry collection is *Environmental Studies*.

ALSO BY MAUREEN DUFFY

MAUREEN DUFFY

Wounds

VINTAGE BOOKS
London

Published by Vintage 2013

2 4 6 8 10 9 7 5 3 1

First published in Great Britain in 1969 by
Hutchinson & Co (Publishers) Ltd

Vintage
Random House, 20 Vauxhall Bridge Road,
London SW1V 2SA

www.vintage-books.co.uk

Addresses for companies within The Random House Group Limited
can be found at: www.randomhouse.co.uk/offices.htm

The Random House Group Limited Reg. No. 954009

A CIP catalogue record for this book
is available from the British Library

ISBN 9780099587361

The Random House Group Limited supports The Forest Stewardship
Council® (FSC®), the leading international forest-certification organisation.
Our books carrying the FSC label are printed on FSC®-certified paper.
FSC is the only forest-certification scheme supported by the leading
environmental organisations, including Greenpeace. Our
paper procurement policy can be found at
www.randomhouse.co.uk/environment

Printed and bound in Great Britain by Clays Ltd, St Ives plc

One

Gently this time he came into her from behind, climbing up through the yielding reaches of soft flesh that drew him in until he lay full length over the undulations of buttock and along the straight back, his mouth against the line of her hair and the heaviness of the cheek turned away from the pillow.

'Am I hurting you?'

'Yes, but I like you to hurt me.'

'Kiss me.'

She raised her head a little so that their mouths could meet and they clung for a long time, unmoving except for the searching of his tongue along the moist ridges of her palate and the sharp definitions of teeth, her own soft live tongue and the beating of quick pulses between their thighs.

'Do you want to turn over?'

'Do you want me to?'

'No.'

He kissed her again, small kisses on mouth and eyes, feeling a frightening tenderness, that would turn in a touch to lust, at her lying so quiescent, at the flattened curve of her breast against the sheet, the passive weight of surrendered flesh, the arms bent under her head reminding him of a crucifixion. With a sudden need to feel her respond and his own urgency, he slid a hand under her body, burrowing between the slack belly and the bed until he touched her with the tip of his finger and heard the quick gasp, the breath indrawn that made him sink his teeth into the folded muscles of neck and shoulders.

Eyes closed she was conscious of his weight, of the sharp pleasure of her bitten flesh and his movement inside her, and

11

the bright impulses that flickered away from his hand, earthing themselves deep in her belly until they ran together in one incandescent sensation that forced her lips open to let out the cries of a small ravaged animal.

'Oh Christ,' he said. 'Christ, darling,' and he was lifted up and flung by the spasm that tore through him and into her, his hands under her hips forcing her closer so that he erupted, broke deep inside her, hearing himself groan and cry out too, short and fierce and hard, and lay spent, fallen across her body like the slain. For some time after there was no movement in the room.

The spade bit into the soil black with the leaf mould she fed into it every autumn, and neatly through the soft pinkness of a worm so that the sundered halves continued to writhe, not realizing they were dead, in a fierce motor activity so counterfeiting life that, for a moment, she thought she had merely parted them in love. But they were quite dead.

'Poor dear creature,' she said, 'Kingy wouldn't have killed you, not meaning to. It's a terrible thing but I have to do it for the sake of the good earth.' The segments writhed reproachfully but were silent. She sheared again with the bright blade, laying the two ghosts under the next mashed clod, its crumbling another testimony to the power of decay. Or was it ghost, she wondered. One half contained the organs that made the intrinsic worminess, the other was just the spasm of sympathy, a broken cadenza prolonging itself in the mind beyond the last heard note. Why did it matter to know which half was which, which serpent veritable and which mirror image? She struck again, smashing home-burrows, earthways, paths, granaries against winter. Innocent uncarnivorous worms. The blade sliced a leaf, cleanly as a fresh-picked runner, that some provident had dragged down to the underworld where now he was perhaps flesh for the vulture ants who would carve sweet minute steaks with their precise mandibles and not even a bone remain. The worms aerated and manured as she did and in the night crept out to make love, ambisextrously, lying swooning lapped together.

'Love, they don't know how to make love. I've lain all night with a woman just content to lie; I was so honoured. And then

that creature offering me money in the ⟨...⟩
money," I said, "when you've learnt to ⟨...⟩
you,' she shook the flat spade at a predatory ⟨...⟩
are with your fancy waistcoat, you're as bad a⟨...⟩
yes, worse, always coming when I'm digging ⟨...⟩
slaughter you do.' The bird cocked a mechanical h⟨...⟩
to the rumblings in the earth where small creatures ⟨...⟩
clockwork through the dark, his eye beaded for ever⟨...⟩
that might be the soil-bred glossy pallor of grub or the ⟨...⟩e
flicker of a wireworm.

Leaves fell, rocking gondolas in the still air, upheld for a
moment by the shallows of mist that washed the garden and
tacking down through sunlight to beach with an audible plop
though they were sucked of substance the greedy tree had
drawn back in self-preservation, sealing them off like weaned
children and finally orphaning them completely. The worms
drew them down tidily convoluted to munch and mulch until
only the skeletal tracery remained. She bent again, spare as an
insect, birdsmall, and the lash of forty years' hard labour cracked
down across the narrow shoulders and back, straightening her
with a twist of pain. 'Love, it's a killing thing and so is this.' She
worked slowly, finishing the bed neat as a nurse, the edges
compass-drawn, shorn precisely out of the grass. 'A killing
thing,' she said again into the mellow garden hung like a ripe
pear on the morning, drew the belt a notch tighter around the
baggy flannels and scraped her bootsoles on the spade, wincing
as an old fork wound jarred in the toe she kept mummified in
animal wool.

'"You have the body of a young girl Miss King," that's what
they said to me at the hospital, and I said to them, "Sir, you'll
pardon me, I am nothing but I have never abused my body in
any way." And then they did fearful things to me, and I was so
ashamed I cried because I'd never been touched by a man
before.' She stabbed the spade into the moist earth, greying as
the crust dried. The robin jerked and picked ferociously among
the ridges. Drawing a pair of secateurs from her pocket she
stepped between the rose bushes, lifting overblown heads and
severing them mercilessly, burying her face in the youth of
buds. 'Is it not wonderful Kingy? Are they not beautiful?' she
chanted, snipping and gathering, tossing the deadheads into a
heap where they broke in falling into a confetti of petals and
laying the buds like sleeping schoolgirls together on the grass.

print billowed toward her between the apple trees, ...dy inside inflating rather than filling it, an anonymous biscuit cardigan attempting to cling and define it. 'A cup of coffee Miss King?'

'You are most kind,' and she bowed a little to her old lady schoolteacher.

'You make the garden so, so . . . ' The broad hands smoothed and patted the flabby arms. 'What should we do without . . . ?'

Kingy stooped to the bunch of young roses. 'Are they not beautiful Miss Williams? Isn't it a fabulous thing the good earth that such creatures as this should come out of it? And then they talk about man; man is nothing, filth. You'll excuse me. I am most true.'

Miss Williams murmured, her eyes travelling vague as the thin sunlight through the garden. 'Beautiful. I must put them in water. Will you take some? After all, you grew them.'

Kingy selected one tight bloom in exchange for the empty cup. 'And now I must away. I will come to you again next week?' It was a formula like all her language, the phrases set counters that she pushed out in well-defined moves, wanting only set answers that she could respond to with the right-coloured piece. No new concept troubled her. There would have been no phrase for it to lurk behind while it insinuated itself like a sprouting weed into a mind set fast as a formal though exotic garden. There were memories as high and brilliant as sunflowers or hollyhocks but everlasting, unchangeable against the stout trellises she had built, and ways between clipped hedges ending always blind like the deliberate confusions of a maze we have designed to divert us from any way out.

Combing her short grey hair with her fingers she put on the stained mac, picked up the canvas shopping bag and limped into the street, Miss Williams murmuring and patting herself at the front door shutting tight on the dim hall where light came chastened through jewelled glass and left no imprint on the red flagged floor. Perhaps Miss Williams hung herself on the coatrack among the other dark-grey weaves until summoned again by the doorbell. Kingy turned her eyes up to the cool pale disk of the sun that let its gaze fall veiled on her pugface. 'I am old and ugly but once I had red hair and pretty teeth and I have been loved by the most handsome women in the world.' Lena walked toward her down the empty street over thirty years, her skin like a white cyclamen, dropping the last silk froth while drums roared and lightning peeled into dark. 'She held my hand in front of them all.'

'I want a cigarette.'

'I want a cigarette,' he imitated, not the words but the syllables of his own heart.

'It doesn't sound a bit like me. How could you love someone who talked like that?' She leaned across him letting the heavy breasts drag across his body, giving him a pleasure he couldn't ask for but awaited, knowing it would come like a free gift or something he had hoarded for and at last been offered out of an open palm, largesse.

'Do you want one?'

'I'll share yours.'

He watched her flick the lighter and draw in. Sometimes he lit it for her. Sometimes he put the smooth cylinder between her lips like another penetration, sometimes in his own mouth and then to hers, a transferred intimacy, so that whatever way her cigarette after love gave him an intense and conscious pleasure and he was never able to accept or light again under different circumstances without that room and their loving and her face, heavy darkened with love as she bent over him filling his vision to the horizon limits and beyond, going on and on soundlessly echoing into infinity, rising in him like a sob blotting out tangible objects, the reality of a present that wasn't immediate because without meaning, composed of flat matt surfaces only that were incapable of reflecting light, of giving pain or pleasure.

And she feeling the intensity of him diminished a little after love drew on the smoke to fill the loss, to soothe her return to herself or to give her the illusion that they had all time, that the external dimension broken by their love had no longer power to march on its own spondaic feet while they lingered outside it with the faculty of children to suspend hours caught in the intense web of their existence, held miraculous and perfect to themselves as spheres of fluid crystal or the stilled act of art.

It had been a hard night, he reminded himself, twisting the glass

15

with a flourish against the wadded cloth. No wonder he felt like death. He'd have to cut down on it though. The occupational hazard of this trade, a veritable industrial disease and many the fine upright man he'd seen glaze and totter over the years, the cheeks veining into a perpetual blush; the furred and stumbling tongue, though they still managed to draw and add up, not able to string a decent sentence together to make a pennorth of sense except for what was running in the two-thirty. He'd have time in a minute to slip out and put a dollar on the Irish horse, on Kerry Boy's nose for old times' sake and luck, while Maura held their thirsts down. They were slow coming in this morning; and too early for the lunches yet. He looked across at her and cocked an eyebrow. She was talking to the flash man, her big breasts resting on the bartop as she leaned, quiet as two full jugs waiting to be picked up. He liked the power of her, the dependability. All the men liked her though she'd no looks: one of the Dublin pigfaces and hair bleached to straw but no tart. You could lie there and be soothed and the arms go round you. Not that he ever, being a happy family man, but they all knew what it was about Maura. There was a painting he'd seen once hung on the school wall when he'd gone up after one of the children, and very surprised he was to see a painting of a pub, and a French one, up in a classroom and a barmaid looking out at you, only not looking, the eyes gone past and beyond or perhaps in. That was it, looking in like Maura did in a slack moment when he'd catch her suddenly, held like the girl in the picture, only she'd been prettier of course. What did they think about at such times? Love was it? Or home? She still had the family back there. Always crossed over, a dutiful daughter, for all the feasts, hung with presents like a stubby Christmas tree.

She nodded back at him. 'Will you put half a crown on for me; the Irish horse. I'll give you the money when you come back.' The flash man creased his paper to a neat tabloid cut to the essentials of the day's runners and smoothed it with coarse-haired fingers. She thought she wouldn't care much for them to be touching her, they were too close to the monkeys in the zoo. She liked a thin white man best, someone who could do with a bit of comforting and wasn't ashamed to admit it like the big thick ones were who needed it just as much but wouldn't take it; always wanting to be humping all over you and never still to cover up they were as weak as newborn kittens inside. She watched Tom's back block out the sunshine in the doorway and then be gone like a blind flung up and her left blinking at the sudden access of light.

'It's a real tip is it, this Kerry Boy?' the flash man was asking.

'More sentimentality like though they say he's a good horse. But I reckon he'll end up hot favourite with all the Irishmen backing him today, him being the only Irish horse running.'

'You stick together worse than the Yids.'

'We do not. Only we know how to breed fine horses. You're a long time finishing that small drink.' She pointed contemptuously at the half-pint glass. The flash man gulped the dregs obediently.

'Had too much last night. Have to take it easy.'

'Are you telling me? Didn't I see you out hardly able to stand on your own two feet?'

'That's because you're unkind to me.'

'Unkind indeed! You can buy me a drink and I must see what they're needing up the end. I can't stand here all morning talking to you. I've me work to do. I'll have a tonic water as it's early yet.' She filled the half deftly and spitefully, her own sure movements an unvoiced criticism of his trembling hands.

Why did she take all the stuffing out of him? He was proud of his little toothbrush taz and elegant white raincoat, the wallet that bulged fivers, and she made them seem nothing. Yet the more she did the more he wanted her. She was no looker but he wanted her. He could have bought anything just to ease him, women in bars all over the city, and did when he couldn't stand it any longer but he always came back to Maura. His bald head sweated with anxiety. What was it that she saw in him that she wouldn't have? She had others he was sure though she never said and neither did they. But she must have. A woman like that couldn't do without and didn't look as if she did either. There was that one last week from the building site, dusty in his overalls, came in at dinnertime and then again in the evening, not speaking to anyone. She kept him well filled up and every time there was a lull she was over there talking very low like to a child or an animal. A whippet of a feller but his hair was too long and another bloody Irishman by the look of him, still with the bog on his boots.

She was glad of the pints of mild she had to pull for the pensioners in the public; sweet stout for the ladies. Well maybe she'd end up like that sitting in a warm corner, sipping to make it last. How did they manage in this country to do on their few ha'pence; not like at home where there was always family around to help you out though they said it was all changing now, getting more like here or America. She noticed it every time she went back: something gone, something taken its place. 'Where's the old man's then, McNeil the grocer's?' she'd ask and be told they'd pulled the whole corner down to make a garage with catchpenny adverts and bright robot pumps on sentry-go.

'You're looking well this morning Mrs. May.'

'Thank you dear. Better for seeing you.' And they would go back to the wobbly wooden table and hard chair spoken to, cheered. There was Wilf bringing up his empty glass for a refill. He'd be off in another half-hour to cook his bite to eat. You could set your clock by his comings and goings.

'Good morning Kingy and how are you this bright morning?' Unzipping a light ale she tilted the glass against the lively froth. Nutty as a fruitcake but harmless until she got too much drink inside her but then that was true of most of us. And what if she did wear men's clothes, what injury did that do anyone?

Kingy laid the rose on the bar. 'Is it not beautiful? Will you do me the honour young woman? Please accept it. I am most true.'

'I haven't a pin dear to fix it to me bosom.'

Kingy unsheathed a small bright dagger from the point of her lapel. 'See a pin and pick it up. I never pass a pin young woman. It could save a life. Will you allow me?' She nipped off a length of stem between accustomed fingers and stripped away the dark gloss of the leaves until a perfect buttonhole remained which she held out to Maura to take. The flash man laughed.

'Will you drink with me man?' Kingy swung to face him. 'Give the man a scotch.' She raised her glass when Maura had measured him a single ignoring his muttered refusal. 'Salut. Your very good health.' Gulping he returned the gesture. The rose rested, a lit butterfly, against the slope of Maura's breast so perfect the fingers tingled to see if it was real or would repel touch with an artificial brittleness.

'Seven to one and half a dollar you owe me. The price is falling all the time.' Tom pushed his way through the flap with two fistfuls of glasses automatically collected in his progress across the bar. He looked back to the oblong of light. Five bob to win on Kerry Boy. The sun fell across sand and sea, and far out an island sullen under a smudge of cloud rowed a dark hull toward him as he ran along the bay, the ridged pools hard and cold even through the horny carapaces of summerbare feet.

He let his mouth travel the white shores of flesh between breast and shoulder, feeling her hand moving in small caresses over his head.

Dead of course, doubly dead having died once then and again when she died though he'd thought he was beyond any more dying except the merely physical and this he would achieve first so no one need ever know he went clockwork about his days. And then she beat him to it and he couldn't die. The body went on tick tock, tick tock, the mechanism whirring, missing beats, wheezing and picking up again. How she'd cosseted him through every chill, and now he took no care of himself until a voice prompted, 'You'd like a tot of rum in hot milk. Do you good.' And obediently he would heat and drink wondering as he did why, to what end since he was dead; keeping him going still like a geranium she'd grown and was proud of, potted and brought indoors to stand in the window while the frost knocked on the glass, and though it never bloomed it was in fine leaf, sucked greedily on the water with five drops of plant food, distilled seaweed, measured accurately into it, and grew taller and thinner, reaching toward a withheld light like his own attenuated time.

A lot of scarecrows all of them when you looked around: the three weird sisters in the corner with their savouring of disaster, who's ill, who's dead like a cartoon from Hogarth, all nose and chin and the idiosyncratic clothing of the old worn not just for protection but as babies are swaddled into security; the two Welshmen, unjovial Celts, all that was left of a depression immigration of sixteen still chattering in their incomprehensibles as if they made a living language though perhaps this was their only converse with the quick this that they had with each other and all other speech was clay-tongued. Then Eddie lamenting his manhood gone with the mumps at forty and all the girls he'd known. 'Four a day for a fortnight and then nothing but beer for a month. My wife was very good. Another woman might have gone off. All I can do is tickle them now.' And Tom, look at Tom with a lovely wife and two boys but going the way of all guv'nors. Coming back from the races in his dogtooths half-cut and carrying on till closing time, the brain pounded insensible as a boxer's under flurries of rounds. He turned from one to the other in his mind rejecting them all; the old girl they called Kingy dead long ago by the look of her, coffined up with memory like him, and the flash man with his eyes blank as stone marbles before the pretty swirled glass ones came in his own Charlie had played with.

Time to be going when it got you like that, seeing everyone in a glass darkly. He took his own jug up to the bar.

'Another, Wilf?'

'Not this journey. I'm off home to cook a bit of dinner. Do a few things in the greenhouse if the weather keeps up.'

'Look out now. No overdoing it. We'll be seeing you later?'

'Oh yes. I'll be in.' He touched a finger to his cap. 'So long er . . . Maura.' He always had trouble with their names.

'See you Wilf.'

Hands pocketed, shoulders consciously back, he went out into the square where the comforting red buses stood at patient attention between trips. The rank diesel fumes made him cough but they were better than horses. Those who were sentimental about them had never known the reek and filth and clatter of the city in those days; the murderous accidents – men and beasts mashed and screaming, slipping on the cobbles in the slime of dung and mud and a thin bone snapped; the soothing voice as you put the narrow muzzle to the quivering head and blew its brains out; the panic roll of the runaway's eyeball before it cut loose, battering a strayed child into the gutter among the cabbage stalks, orange papers, blown litter of millions of untidy lives, lived hastily and thrown away. The waste, the waste. He looked along the orderly street where cars and pedestrians moved in easy geometry and saw the naphtha flares bloom through the gas-green fog, the old inferno of the High Street on a Saturday night.

And going into battle with them, clinging to a stirrup iron as they trotted army-trained to robots, the boot you had buffed last evening level with your cheek; the mechanized gambit of lead toys but they were flesh and died like flesh under

bombardment. Had to do away with them of course, ceremonial purposes only. Yet at first the officers wouldn't let them
go: their pride, their manhood, their tradition. That was how
an officer and gent died, shot down like an aunt sally upright on
horseback. The bitter small hours spent polishing and grooming till the beast seemed cast in bronze and the man to go with it,
accoutred for death as he'd have met his mistress, sleeked and
ardent in white kid gloves. Only the mistress was some French
tart back of the line who didn't need to be wooed only bought.
Ha, ha among the strumpets. You always knew the poor
buggers of infantry cut down in a cavalry charge, slashed about
the head as though beaten with a riding crop.

Opening the door with the heavy key he bowed into the cold
gloom of the passage. Whoever had built them hadn't meant
you to die of a rush of daylight. When the room doors were shut
upstairs and down, to step in out of the street was to fall down a
well or to find yourself suddenly at the bottom looking up into
the blackness of the landing. He stood quite still, the door
closed behind him, feeling the familiarity reach out for him,
and nothing moved or sounded beyond his own piping chest
where the phlegm bubbled among the tubes, narrowing the
airways into mucus-fingered stops. They had laughed at his
musical box to avert her fear and it ran in his head, that
laughter, whenever he was silent listening to his breath.

He went through into the kitchen, into the half-light that
topped next door's fence and trickled through the window, and
began the ritual of making himself eat. First you put on the
kettle and then you take the newspaper-wrapped bloaters from
the table where there should have been a note with directions,
would have been in her regular hand, the school-board
copperplate in blue biro lacing the lined page with her concern,
unwrap them on the scrupulously white enamel draining board,
saw through the bony mask of dried head, the eyes smoke-bur-
nished and flattened to a cipher, with a knife honed to bayonet
sharpness on the roughened edge of the sink, bring down the
black frying pan heavy as a trenching tool that you had wielded
as a talisman, carried on your back for four years and so home,
half-fill with white blobs of lard and seethe on the gas ring after
the kettle, the brewing-up, the solace of steam and habit.

When he had eaten, finicking between the bones that would
choke him to a desired death for the soft wedges of tangy
meat, oak-cured at Ward's still, he unlatched the door into the

21

back yard and stood in the quiet of the lavatory listening to a blackbird singing from the high sycamore in the playground where they had both gone to school, and his own small fountain spurting a clean continuo onto the Plimsoll line at the back of the pan. Behind him the daddy longlegses who moved in with early summer waited like spindly tables that might scuttle across the room at any moment. He should kill them. They laid leather jackets that ate the plant roots, bulb and tuber, but he couldn't. Motionless, they never stirred while you were in there, they watched, heard the door clang to and gave an insect sigh, perhaps restrung the wire legs. What did they eat, or did their pared substance need almost no sustaining like his own? He didn't know quite where they came in the life cycle, larva, pupa, adult. Perhaps they were merely living out the summer waiting to die in the first scything of frost. He shook off the last thin drops, soothed the foreskin into place and adjusted his person as the notices always read implying that that was all there was to you.

Everything grew less well now that the ground wasn't properly turned. He raked it as best he could, stirring the topsoil, but he preferred the greenhouse. She had dug with energy and conviction. Digging made him cough and wheeze. He had dug and dug too long ago. They had been human moles among their earthworks, blinking in the gunflashes, palled day after day with smoke until their eyes could no longer take full light. He sieved the fine black flour of potting compost through his fingers. It brushed off leaving no trace; didn't cling like mud and clay yet nourished delicate seedlings, the innocent strength of bulbs. He would sleep a little and then eat a bit of tea and out to the Sugarloaf for the evening session. The nights were drawing in. Soon he would be going out in the dark.

'Sleep,' she said, 'if only we could sleep now.'

'Soon,' he said, 'make it soon.' He lifted a tail of damp hair from her ear, hair that had still the fineness and softness of a child's, and buried his face in the silk mesh drawing in the savour of it. 'Why is it so necessary to sleep together? Not necessary,' he corrected quickly in case she should feel it as a demand, something she should satisfy, a threat. 'I mean important. What is it about sleeping together?'

'The relaxation I suppose.' She moved her hands to and fro across his back as she spoke, in counterpoint to her thoughts. 'The unconscious entwining as well as the conscious.' He thought how he had held her while she slept, how if there was ever greater sweetness than their lovemaking it had been that time when she had stirred in the night. She had put her mouth, pouting full with sleep, to his and murmured, 'Darling,' and he had kissed her and held her while his wanting beat and beat against the warm flesh of her belly and he had fought it for her rest. He had slept catnapping, waked and winked again, unwilling to lose a moment of her and in the grey of morning they had made love again very softly, the warmth flowing between them as if they were bedded in swansdown until they could no longer tell who took or who gave, transfusing into each other without distinction, their mouths enfolding as she enfolded him.

And shouldered through the door with a swagger as if it was closed and he had to assert himself against it though he knew it was really the turned white adult faces he was thrusting against as he'd seen them do in the Westerns, confronting a full saloon, the slid bottle, 'Take a drink stranger,' and the need to prove himself against the natives. R U 18 stared back from the tactful cartoon above the bar.

They didn't usually go into the saloon, didn't much frequent the pubs in this part anyway, and when they did it was always the roughest and the public bar where they stood self-conscious among the overalls in their round narrow-brimmed black hats and pegtop trousers. They were hicks, newcomers, and he despised them from his city-bred soul, hitching the narrowest jeans he could shrink to his long bones against his hard round buttocks to feel the cling of them. He hated their overconfident laughter, the voices that he had once heard described as a seal with a mouthful of galoshes, the camaraderie he didn't recognize in himself. Almost inaudible he asked for ten Cadets, aware that the barmaid had called him dear and unsure whether to be affronted or not. Going back was even harder against the faces that swivelled automatically to the bar even when they didn't see it, as eyes will focus on a grate though empty of fire, but he breasted them strongly with elbows bent arrogant as wings, his hands in the high anorak pockets, dark face set in blank nonchalance.

'You don't get many of them coming in here,' Tom said.

'No, thank Christ.' The flash man wiped his wet lips on the back of his hand once, twice.

'Ah he was just a kid and the money's all the same colour.' The flash man sighed. Whatever he said today she put him down.

He picked the bike off the railings and swung his leg ostentatiously straight over the saddle, drove hard down, left, right, his head low over the shining oxbow of the handlebars, feeling his thighs and calves taut and throbbing with the excitement of the thrust until the bike swung into the one-way system and along the common, a capsule in orbit, gyrating on an invisible thread round the blanched grass, faster, faster, dizzying him as he overtook cars; and the little world of lunchtime play where the office girls bit into sandwiches and the boys tussled with a ball for display eddied through his speed, figures through smoke. Sweat gathered at the roots of his hair and threatened his eyes until he ducked his head across the blue sleeve marking a deep stain. The tension faded from his throat leaving a retching emptiness. The capsule slowed and plummeted. What could he do now? Far out over the grass dark figures laughed and leapt at a game of cricket. He saw the short fierce run-up, the doubled legs, the swung parabola of the arm and flung ball, the batsman step to attention and the wild crying and jumping drive him out. Even without the oblong daguerrotypes of their heads patterning his own on the white sky that crying would have betrayed them.

'When we are too old to make love,' she said, 'I shall teach you formal logic and we can play at that all evening.'

'When we are too old to make love,' he said, 'I shall die,' answering with the heart's precise logic.

'Suppose we couldn't for some reason? I mean, suppose it went?'

'You mean you didn't want to?' Once, in the beginning, walking along an anonymous street, when he hadn't been concerned that it should last, he had been struck with the lightning and irresistible knowledge that seeing her across the room in ten years time he would turn sick with wanting her. 'Do you think it might?'

'It's a bit frightening. It's so strong that you wonder if it can last.'

'Whether it will burn itself out?' he asked calmly, trying to choke the panic that clawed at his throat.

'Yes.'

'If you ever don't want to I shall just hang on. I shall be very . . . ' he searched about for a neutral word, 'distressed but I love you, all of you, and I shall wait for it to come back. If it's right it will come back.' Like someone who winds a scarf around the horse's head to lead it out of the blazing stable afraid of the flailing hoof that will destroy both in a welter of fire, he wondered at his own strength when he knew that sometimes alone he was weak as a half-drowned rat with need and lack of her, struggling to the side of the water butt, getting a nose, a frantic paw over the rim and pushed down again to begin the treading insubstantial water, the abyss beneath; the feeble paddling, conviction slipping fluid between his fingers; drowning in the fear that he had invented her love for him, that it would be suddenly taken from under him and he sink into nothingness. It was his solitary vice. He had only to hear her voice on the telephone, begin to drive toward her through the log roll of traffic, and he became strong. Apart he no longer existed in any sense that he was willing to recognize as existence. Was it the same for her? Probably not, he thought. Their abnegation, their suffering had a different quality. Absence was something she would carry about diffused through her. He saw it running slow and thick in her veins.

'I feel it as much as you do,' she had said once, 'but I don't make such a fuss.'

He did make a fuss. Savagely he fought himself, and swore; and got drunk and rang inopportunely, incoherently, angry and ashamed at himself, his lack of control. He would have torn down walls, brick and bar, to reach her. He saw himself as weak, demanding, and despised his lack of patience. In the same way his physical need was fierce, insistent; leapt up with the brilliance of an exploding rocket scattering stars, soaring impetuously so that he was afraid of driving her away with his urgency and beat upon her with kisses until she should say, 'Take me to bed.' He needed her to want him, not that he should have to force but that it should jump between them, a spark leaping the gap, arching between their polarities and welding their flesh into one demanding whole. His hand slid down over the slight mound to part her thighs, opening the small secret kingdom he made his own.

This country stank from the top of its bald head to the soles of its lily-white feet, feet of clay, muddy from the running murk of the weeping sky, pus white of putrefaction from the wet, the ooze of the lowering clouds over the blackened walls, and today when the sun do shine veiled as if ashamed of itself. Putrefaction! She spat it delightedly among the long brown fibrous roots of the yams as she knived them out of their overcoats. It had come to her first out of a newspaper wrapping describing a corpse neglected in a room for months. 'Putrefaction had already set in,' and she had gone to the paperback dictionary among the half-dozen tattered books that Stuart was forbidden to draw in parked on top of the wooden chest that had once been out of his reach, and thumbed through: '*n*. process of putrefying; rotting matter.' 'Set in' was good too with its overtones of a jelly left to liquefy instead of harden.

It was a strange language this English English or rather composite of languages, a compote of fruits as they'd read on the menu of the Tudor Restaurant where she'd taken Stuart for the 3/6d lunch on their day out to Canterbury. He had said they should see the cathedral and she had half understood that he would take them but it hadn't happened and in the end she had taken the boy herself. How they all stared politely, hiddenly, over their roast meat that was like shavings of cheap dark cardboard and the mush of cabbage, the unyielding crust of dried potatoes that had calcified about emptiness, with cold calm, the eyes swivelling and then away if you tried to catch them. So kind, so polite these English that at first you were deceived that it might mean something more until you learned that, like the potatoes, there was nothing behind. Sometimes in a winter morning when she came into the fug of Alec huddled under his blankets in the kitchen, a crescent of black froth pushed up on the pillow the only sign of his life in the bed, the bowl left in the sink overnight would have a very thin rind of ice. When you tried to pick it up it dissolved and slid away from the warmth of your fingers while leaving them with a sensation of slight numbness, rejection. That was how they were these people. They slid away remote behind their glazed blue eyes, that drew you snakily, sneakily, and struck you down while you stared back with the brown brooding moistness of a mesmerized rabbit, your own held dark eyes pierced and melting, and behind their words that were sharp and cold, untextured, adding no richness of layered colour but defined, precisioned, tooled so that the language they spoke didn't give themselves, wasn't offered out of them in generosity, the sounds tumbling, breaking into coloured bubbles, the punctuation cries of love or pain, but etched them age, class, sex and left you to make your bid because you had to and then they would slide away.

'What is it Mummy, compote?'

'I don't know my dear.' Composed, composition, compost, composite. 'But if it's fruit, it's fruit.' It was sour plums and apple stained black in stewed proximity, made edible only by the sweet vomit of custard topping.

Winter was coming again. She dreaded it now, knowing the feel of it, apprehending it in the added glaciation of the tap water as she sluiced the peeled yams. They never imagined at home. They'd heard of course but it was a myth and suspect; a ruse to keep you sweating at home for a pound a month; nothing could be like that. You couldn't conceive that the sun would go, lost for weeks behind the piled muck of cloud like dirty snow, that you would get up in dark and live a few hours in twilight and so into dark. Down here it was worse of course. In summer a little light came through the net you had to put up at the front-room window to catch the eyes peering down into your life, and the whole of the kitchen window was above ground, looking onto the yard and the railway line where the children would play against all cautioning, but in winter the electric light burned all day when she was off duty, gobbling at shillings. He had said the meter was fixed, that the landlord took a rake-off every time he emptied it. Sometimes it even refused the proffered shilling or rather swallowed it down and gave nothing back. Then she beat it with a stick in rage. Last time he had come it had refused light and, knowing he was coming, she screamed and struck it again and again till the girl upstairs had come running to see if she was hurt and she had been ashamed to let those people who were nothing but tramps see her reduced to their level of frustration and despair, and its animal expression. She heard them at night, the blows and cries, the inevitable pounding reconciliation. The girl was pregnant again. The three-year-old, snotty-nosed and snivelling, clung, thumb in mouth, to her skirts.

How she hated a whimpering child. Stuart whimpered, cried too easily for a boy. Alec grew impatient with him and punched him, and he cried again. In the night he fretted in his dreams as a dog does, pummelling her with his feet and fists, desperately fighting back some playground torment while she stared at the rectangle of thick grey on the dense black, imagining the window, the way out, wondering if the stirring was a rat or just Alec turning on the other side of the wall. When she had shown him the holes in the floorboards he had said they should nail pieces of hardboard over them to keep the draughts down. He had said he would like to do it but it hadn't been done. He had said, had said.

Perhaps she was too old for him. She put the pan of yams to simmer gently and went through into the other room, passing below the offending meter that began its furious gallop as soon as she switched on the light. She looked at herself in the staring glass of the wardrobe. Now she no longer modelled for Abraham, the grey began to grizzle the roots at her temples like an old dog's flecked muzzle, a thin silver ribbon outlining her face. She still had her hair straightened. Once she'd said, 'I couldn't have that hair,' when he'd asked. 'But I'm not old,' she murmured at the glass. 'Plenty men give their eyes for me.' She traced the charcoal line across the bridge of her nose with a slim forefinger. All her family had it like a brand. He had said too, 'It'll be better when we're all coffee-coloured.' So it wasn't that, not that. She really believed it wasn't that.

The stark ugliness of the landlord's furniture was naked in the harshness of the mirror: the kicked double bed, the grimed sagging armchair, the scabbed and leprous chest, all stained and battered by a succession of uncaring, uncared-for tenants. Only she had to put up with it, this inheritance, because she had no man to fight for her. Upstairs they had had new curtains and a three-piece suite last Christmas because the man had threatened to smash the collector's white face in. The room seemed crowded and yet bleak; the fireplace a gaping black gullet in its iron porch. Soon it would be time to go to the hospital. She was on late duty this week. Why hadn't Alec come back? She begged he would be in before Stuart came home in

28

the afternoon. It was better when he was at the college all day, then hunger drove him back. Halfdays were all very well but she knew how they dragged for him. He would be out on his bike, circling, circling, unwilling to spend an afternoon cooped in the squalid tomb of their living, squandering his paper-round money on cigarettes and bottles of Coke, parleying to the girls. Please God he don't get one pregnant. Please God he finish at the college so he can go anywhere, be anything. Go back and get a fine job out of this damn country where you nothing but dirt, get treat like dirt. Only the dying glad for you, glad for you to wash them and feed them and pot them. Only they smile and give you kind words.

'The trouble is,' he said, 'I just can't leave you alone.'

'And do you think I want you to? Don't you know how much pleasure it gives me just that fact that you can't? Don't you know how I want you there all the time?' She let the words move over him like caresses and because this was what he wanted, what he needed to be told, he punctuated the phrases with soft kisses, thinking how her very syllables were tactile as gestures. 'I'm glad we're older. If we'd been young, adolescents still, we wouldn't have been ready for each other. When you're very young you think you've got time to play. It's all in front of you. We know that's not true for us.'

'I'm glad too,' he said aware of the interweaving of their voices, 'because it gives us a greater . . . oh, what I can only call the intensity of maturity. It's not a very good phrase perhaps.'

'It's like having a child. When you're young you're often not psychologically ready for it and by the time you are your body is almost beyond it.'

He traced the marbled course of a vein in the full white breast. 'Would you have liked to be pregnant by me?'

'Would you have liked it?'

'Sometimes when I'm inside you I can see it so clearly as if I were planting a seed in the wall of your flesh. It's so strong that image it's almost as if I could watch it grow. Yes, of course I'd like it; so much I can't even say, put it into the right words.'

'I would have liked it too; so much I'd be pregnant by you all the time and that'd ruin our love life. Then you'd complain. There's nothing like pregnancy and children for taking up lovers' time.' Gently she led him over the flawed surface of their wanting, easing their denial into a shared strength that was beyond bitterness and fretting, where otherwise he might have stumbled and torn himself on the sharpness of the loss.

'Sweet,' he said, 'you are so sweet you make everything whole.'

'My occupation is staying alive,' the eyes bright with tenacity, consumed white walls, humped beds, the tree beyond her window, the order of her locker top, the chintz curtaining half drawn about the bed, her throne. 'Gay, that's it. I like that design. Clean and cheerful. I've always liked things clean and cheerful.'

'Now Mrs. Robson, it's time for you medicine. You looking very smart today.' The chocolate hand reached out with a small glass of chalky liquid. She had hated them at first, recoiling with the inbred disgust of her generation. On Empire Day as children they had sat in the school hall, crosslegged, boys on one side, girls on the other, while the headmistress talked to them about the poor ignorant black people over the sea who rubbed dust in their hair and hung animal teeth on their bodies, ivory on ebony, and who looked up to us like children because we were so much more advanced. 'As you look up to your parents and teachers.' But why hadn't they advanced? Because they were different. She looked at her own doll hands so white and neat and imagined the thick black native sausages, coarse with pounding meal and rubbing down hides, shuddered over the flyblown sores under the festering sun.

Her father's little fairy, she played and sang and painted flowers for him while the family clapped and chattered admiringly. She saw herself in her party flounces so sweet and clean, an icing figure skating the pink-and-white sugar surface of her birthday cake under the eight dancing candles stilled a moment, multiplied in the bent watching eyes of her aunts and uncles before she blew them all out with pouting red lips. Black lips were made of rubber, blubber. What would it be like to kiss? Her mind skipped away, fragile as a glass-hoofed fawn, from the gross suggestion. And two of them mouth to mouth? Hovering round the forbidden thought she felt its hot impulse lick out at her and drew back.

30

On the way to school the children leapt from paving stone to stone, 'Tread on the black lines marry a black man,' and thrilled when they toppled. It couldn't be true. No one could make you. But there was God who was an old gentleman of great power like Grandfather for whom she had to be quiet and who was not seduced by her prattle, and there was the Lady Fortune who was etched blackly over the drawing-room mantelpiece. God was blamed for the death of her elder brother who had been taken by Him as a six-day baby, and Fortune for the failure of Uncle William's boot factory. There was no being sure with those two. God was placated every Sunday at long doleful services and Sunday school. Missionaries were offered as sacrifices and your collection ha'pennies went to provide them, and clothes for the black men and women. Fortune seemed content with crossed fingers. Once in a leaflet, handed to her with her leather hymn book, thanking them for their generous provision, she had seen boys and girls before and after showing what the ha'pennies had achieved. There were big black girls, and not so big boys but quite big enough, all glossily naked, the breasts of the girls young and proud; the boys with a little dangling collection of penis and balls slung in adornment at the apex of their smooth oval bellies. That was before. After they had looked like the boys and girls who sat all around her on the splintery floor, except for their large impenetrable features. She knew that the big girls in top class had swellings under the gathered yokes of their pinafores. Did this mean that the little boys crosslegged on the other side of the hall had their own bagsful that nested against the cold boards between their open knees under the baggy knickers. She drew her own long skirt down further over the polished tips of her boots to hide all trace of petticoats.

Mrs. Robson pulled a face over the chalky fluid and took herself a glacier mint from the top drawer of her locker. The slimness of brown fingers had startled her at first. The indigo smoothness, proffering glass or thermometer with the firmly spatulate nails in café au lait, fascinated her so that she was forced to look hard and then away quickly because you mustn't hurt their feelings by staring. And they weren't really black but a definite chocolate, bitter plain chocolate on top and then the palms a delicate sepia milk. She had a passion for chocolate. She imagined her own hands made of that white blend she so

31

loved, luxurious and quite artificial so that she felt deliciously wicked with every bite.

Perhaps the minister would come to see her this afternoon. Taking the hand mirror from her little bag, everything she owned had to be small, dainty as herself, she added two deft blushes and redrew the thin lips in carmine. She would ask him about evolution and the Garden of Eden. With thumb and forefinger Mrs. Robson pinched her fringe into devilish curls. The new rinse she had had before coming in had given the sparse hair, 'fine' mother had called it, more body. She must look smart and alert. No one should pity her. There would be no tale to bear back of the poor old thing, and how down and frail she seemed, to those forked tongues in the choir, the ladies she had bullied and cajoled week by week for fifteen years until they were in demand everywhere for their cheery programmes of songs and recitations, not to mention Mrs. Pullinger who told jokes and whistled.

> When the red red robin
> Comes bob, bob, bobbing along,

Mrs. Robson hummed to herself. She would have liked to sing out loud.

> Wake up, wake up you sleepy head,
> Get up, get up, get out of bed.
> Live, laugh, love and be happy . . .

only to see them all leap up in their nightgowns. A pity the men and women were kept apart just like they'd been at school. Some of them in her ward were so crotchety and there was one poor thing she was sure was senile and had to have a feeder like a baby, sucking through the spout while the nurse wheedled and tilted and even then she dribbled. If it came to that she'd die of shame. Please God she went clean and wholesome. Except that she wasn't going. It was just a check-up. She felt fine really, brighter than any of them; could have jumped out of the nest of bedclothes where she perched chirping and preening and danced the twist up the polished aisle of the ward, and they'd all have gathered round from men's orthopaedic next door, on their crutches and in their wheelchairs, and cheered and clapped like they used to when she'd sung 'Where'er You Walk' on a musical evening at home and all the young men leaned forward in their seats, hung on every note, so pure and high her notes, till you could hear their held breath let go in one long sigh before the applause broke. Talented, she'd always been talented, could have been anything if only she'd married a man with more push. Could have been Prime Minister's wife, presided at banquets, met the Queen.

Sometimes in secret, before the long mirror in her one-room flat high up in the concrete block where the wind wailed between the matchbox balconies like a dervish, she'd practised her curtsey so that it didn't rust on her; not the nimble bob of childhood but a more sedate seventy-year-old sinking. One day the Queen might come to visit them, she often did, you saw her on television, and she would be ready with the kettle boiling. 'You must see our liveliest inhabitant,' and they would knock on Mrs. Robson's door. How would Emmie in number seven curtsey with her wooden leg? She would have to duck her head, perhaps bend a little in a stiff bow. Supposing no one had told them, Her Majesty had decided on an impromptu visit outside the official schedule? Hetta Robson would be ready, lived in hourly expectation of the descent of the mighty, but Emmie might be resting, her stump on the footstool, the metal shin and foot at ease in the corner. The Queen would pass by while she swung to buckle it on and sit down to tea with Hetta, admire the gay flowered curtains, the white paint and primrose walls, so clean, the tasteful touches of colour in ornament and scatter cushion and the two big prints of *Spring Among the Bluebells* and *Winter Sunset* that she had had reframed in white out of their heavy wooden mounts. Oh she couldn't abide anything dark and old.

'It's always,' he said, 'quite different every time. At least it is for me. Do you feel that?'

'Yes.' She let the word drop slowly, quietly, almost without articulation, a murmur between them. 'With other people I've always liked the first time best but with us that's not so. Why is that?'

'You may not like this and I may be quite wrong but perhaps with other people it was to satisfy a quick appetite and once that was done that was that. With us the first time is just taking the edge off because we want each other so much. Then as we go on we go deeper as though we were stripping away layers from ourselves. Does that make sense?'

It makes very good sense.' She sat up and leaned across him. 'I want a drink.'

'Greedy. You're full of wants,' he teased and moved the palm of his hand down the length of her back as if stroking a cat.

'You're coming between me and my drink. Do you want some?'

'Maybe I do. Maybe I'm just jealous.' Putting his finger into the sweet-sour wine he traced round the pink nipple that had the innocent perfection of a Rubens breast and then drew it in with lips and tongue. 'That's how I like my drink.'

Passing the hospital always gave him the jitters. Dear heart! The local legends had it you only went in there to die. Such a beautiful piece of architecture too. You could see the patients walking about inside through the long fine proportions of the windows, perfect picture frame, the old boys sitting on each other's beds in blue-striped pyjamas playing cards, poker no doubt, and gossiping as though they didn't know it was the last act. It would make a fabulous play if only someone could write it. It wasn't exactly the kind of thing you could improvise. Whatever Henry said, improvisation, like masturbation, had its limitations. When it came to the real thing you needed something more solid to go on. Someone had to write the dialogue and you couldn't make do with a couple of grunts and a firm handshake. Perhaps he was old-fashioned, out of touch, but if he was he was and there was nothing he could do about it. He was just a sucker for a jutting pros arch, preferably with cupids and that old auntie Queen Anne presiding over the orgy. It was the illusion of overlooking, the eye to the keyhole that he had to have every time. A born voyeur, that was it, a vicarious liver who might as well learn to shake down with himself. Still it was better than ordinary peeping tomfoolery. After all he was the prime mover, made it all happen, caused it to be framed, formal, knowing exactly what would come next, dictating every gesture, nuance, as a lover does, and sat in the third-row stalls, active and passive together, watching, directing. And that was the whole point in back of it all as that curious transatlantic euphemism had it. When it came to the climax he wasn't there.

First nights had him up in the dress circle above it, looking down, the eye precise, uninvolved. So he should settle for sex and art and leave love to the innocent because he would never be old enough to be innocent. His paintbox and toy train would have to do him instead: the subterfuges and pretends of childhood.

For a moment he poised on the edge of the pavement to let the traffic ease. He would cross onto the commonside and walk along the grass verge where he could watch the children running far out as though the grass, nibbled short by the summer and the authority's tractor mowers, were sand and the distant surge of heavy green water not leaves. Art had its compensations, might even turn out to be all there was in the end, and he might have wasted a lot of time with his nose pressed enviously to the glass observing the adults. One could attempt an art of sex and when the performance failed write it off, put it down to experiment, and there would be no bad notices, no incisive perceptive reviewing to confirm it had all been a harrowing mistake, not flowered into the timeless but an exotic that faded overnight and shrivelled when one looked at the face beside one in the morning, doubtless with its mouth open and blackheads seeding the clefts of the nostrils, and couldn't huddle it into its really rather steamy clothes and out of the door fast enough, murmuring, 'Sweet boy, flower, do come again,' with the expected lustful narrowing of the eyes. Not for nothing five years as juvenile lead at Scarborough rep, that loathsome provincial drag.

'London thou art of townes a per se.' Where else would you get such variety of scene in the walk from station to home. He could have taken a cab but he preferred foot. It kept him in trim, was good for the pod you always started to develop as soon as you got off the boards and onto your arse. On a day like this all the world was abroad. One could never cram it all in, that was the trouble, not into one evening's pleasure. Even a five-acter with intervals couldn't compass it. He sighed over the human limitation, a dallying exhalation that wouldn't have changed a thing since he needed this frisson of sadness to give bite to pleasures that will ever cloy. Eternally restless that was it like the soul that would only find peace in God but meanwhile had the hell of a life looking. Make me chaste but not yet.

It was time he gave another party. The last one was a wild success. If only he could be sure that nothing had escaped him, that there was no little bit of business the actors had got away with impromptu, out of reach of his guiding touch. Parties after all were only the sublime opportunity to play impresario: assemble the cast and force them to perform, offer them lines they had to pick up, direct their every action. 'Dear heart, you must meet . . . I've been longing to bring you two together for simply ages,' and then watch them flounder or catch fire while he walked away smacking his lips over the weeks of pleasure that would follow, manipulating, speculating as he nursed the little tragicomedy through its run. The only worrying thought was that sometimes they escaped him, began to speak their own words, took cues from each other and went away to rehearse together in secret. Then he couldn't be sure that it folded when he had had enough of it. With his genius for casting there might be couples all over London that he had brought together whispering into each other's eyes to the silent applause of the gods. Or laughter. You could never be sure which. Definitely he must have another party. A pity that fool Leo had had to knock someone down driving home. It did rather take the edge off things.

He poised himself again on the pavement edge, a plump rook in his dark overcoat, staring across at his own front door, and then stepped back smartly from the onslaught of a driven bike with set brown face pitched low between the gleaming horns. Admiring he watched the round buttocks piston up and down and mentally shaped his hands about the polished wood of dark muscles. The face was familiar. Then he had it in the half-light of a December morning, shamed but defiant. 'I am the paper boy.' No, not paper. Any substance but that: gunmetal, ebony, plastic even. The figure was nearly out of sight now into the one-way stream. There must be a line, a walk-on that could be arranged. It was time someone revived *The Emperor Jones*. He could just hear Henry, 'But Christopher, a boy off the street. You're not budding a starlet you know. The days of Diaghilev are over. And you don't know where he's been.'

'I've never used sex before to get to know someone.' She said it quite deliberately, anticipating his hurt but driven by the ruthless honesty they had made a pact between them.

'Do we use it or does it use us?' Wincing he drew the inversion over the wound and pressed it down like lint to absorb the pain.

'It doesn't matter which way it is, does it?' And then fiercely, 'I will never mitigate anything for you. You are perfect. You must be perfect.'

And he felt the raw edges of torn flesh sutured together in pride that she expected so much of him and nothing less would do.

'I've never been so conscious before either, of what I was doing and why,' she went on.

'I want us to be conscious, to understand each other and ourselves.' He knew the limitation in himself that he had barked against so often before leaving him pocked with the scars of old abrasions: the inability to become one with another person, the keeping apart of his own ego for fear of losing it or of having it rejected which was the same thing like a child with a favourite toy. 'You have all of me,' he said. 'There isn't any more.'

'I know.'

They had lived there for well over a hundred years by his reckoning. Would it be great-grandmother or grandmother who'd sold watercress when the beds of hot green stretched down to the river across the marshes and the small hills were clothed in lavender? There had been Rowes there as long as they could go back but there wouldn't be any more. He'd been the only boy in his generation and he and Eva had had just the one girl before they'd decided to go their separate ways. And now? His mind backed off the thought. A lunchtime drink was meant to stiffen you, not have you buckling at the knees.

> I always rise up early
> My creases for to sell.
> Oh no sir, I'm not lonely.
> They call me the watercrease girl.

His mother had always sung it at family parties, hummed it over the tin bath in the back yard as she slapped and drubbed the washing on the board. He wished he had the gift of singing, could open his mouth and make a great noise that held all the sadness of the human condition and would let his own out in one long wail rising and falling with the contractions of the heart. There were old women used to be able to do it, open up their lungs on a Saturday night to a full house in the strident

37

nasal cockney soprano and bring a lump to your throat as they exhorted Kathleen or the little boy that Santa Claus forgot to be patient for there was nothing else, all said and done, but patience. No kicking achieved anything, only steady negotiation as he had always found. 'A long job,' they would all sigh and shake their heads. 'Send Rowe,' who always said 'Sir' and held his hands together waiting while they fumed on the other side of the desk and said, 'Look here Rowe, you can't expect . . . ' and he didn't but waited, not knowing the root of expectation only that he was sitting there and it wasn't up to him to lead revolutions but to get sixpence on an hour and special concessions for those who worked long and dirty, who tended the purifiers, watching blurred dials through the night while the rest of the city slept and the gas lay silent under the pavements, called on only by shift workers coming home for a cup of tea, hospitals and suicides. And he was back again on his own particular treadmill, nine to five and overtime as well to all hours that was paid in double grief as dusk came and the minutes wore on till it was time to sit by the bedside finding bright things to say to a pretty girl who had danced like a dream and stood to lose both legs because of some drunken bugger, and was his daughter, all he had to show for a lifetime except a price haggled over here, a bonus upped there for the benefit of others while his own flesh and blood he could do nothing for, next to nothing except hold a limp hand and say calm things in his negotiating voice that held men from the edge of bitterness and haste, and was all he could offer this girl he didn't know but loved achingly. How could you know anyone so close? Management he knew and the two boys who shuffled up to him as the metal door clanged into the gates. He knew their wants, read them straight out of their eyes. Concessions, a case taken up. But those other eyes on the pillow asked something he couldn't give though he would have bargained and fought for it, given his life for it if he'd been let, traded all his years of experience for the right thing to say this time, and could only wait, as he always had, hands held together, saying 'Sir' to the surgeon as if he had power to say yes or no when reason told him a doctor was only another negotiator, keeping his head, his fingers from trembling, himself from asking more of the complex of blood and tissue than it could give.

They all knew of course, said, 'Sorry for your trouble mate,' before they began on the recital of their own. He didn't expect more, had never offered coin higher than copper that could be handled back and forth without anyone feeling he was being bought or bribed: dull flat words that fell heavy from giver to receiver and expected no interest as the flights of silver or gold would have done. 'The faithful shop steward,' he had once been called, and he had ducked his small narrow head on its thin neck like a questing tortoise in agreement with the joke, avoiding the over-bright eyes of the lank-haired young conference delegate who would go a long way and whose speech, more intricate than the maze of pipes that fed the big tank, had left him blundering among the syllables in dumbfounded admiration.

'Don't move,' she said, 'I like to feel you there on top of me.'

'At first I wasn't sure if you would. If you'd feel it was domination, arrogance.'

'I wasn't sure either. But I don't feel any of that with you, at least without any resentment. I suppose somewhere there must be some aggressiveness, some irony in my love for you because there always is but I don't feel it. Only love, very simple, pure love.'

A fly zizzed frantically against the pane, impelled by autumn sunlight and the heat of the forcing glass, and then dropped to the sill silent where it preened iridescent wings between its front legs, stroking, combing to a new strength for a second assault. Outside there were multiple dangers, webs to blunder into, stout as it was, hawk eyes that might pounce. But it wanted out. Watching it Gliston felt himself slipping into a daze in the heat of the parlour. His jaw ached with suppressed yawns. The fogging webs of his friends' and colleagues' illogic that would enmesh him while they paralyzed and sucked him dry hung in the smoke-rank air like tattered battleflags in a cathedral, and the predatory enemy waited to plummet down on every weak point. He struggled to pull himself together, fought back the lapping somnolence; shook his head as if he had water in his ears to stay alert.

Gliston was getting fat. Facing the word squarely he refused to equivocate with stout or plump. All these official dinners, jovial lunches were fleshing him thick. That was what did for mayors, the apathy of overweight or a coronary. Would he be too heavy to rise in the end? Had a lifetime in politics knackered him so that he was just an old tomcat, neutered and running to flab? At this hour in the afternoon it all hung as heavy around his neck as the borough chain of office and he wondered what he had ever achieved. A good man in committee, a handler, but did it, in the long run, make any difference the haggling over this and that point of order? Everyone thought you were in it for the prestige and in a sense that was true of the beginning. Some of them were driven by it to the end. But it had died early for him. What remained was the feeling of being caught, of what else could he do, especially when, in honesty, he had to admit that he did it better than most.

Percy was holding forth now in a voice monotonous as the resumed buzz of wings. He had reached thirdly. Fourthly and finally were yet to be plodded through and even then no one would be any the wiser. How had he got onto the planning committee? Long service and a spasm of inertia on Gliston's part. Anyway in a few months' time they would be swallowed up by the monolith borough down the road. Their autonomy would go. It wasn't what John Burns had meant when he'd spoken of a London patriotism. Once there'd been a pride of locality that had made the L.C.C. a United Nations. Now the units were so large, the old names gone into anonymity, even the Town Hall itself was to be abandoned under centralization, used only to house Friday Music Hall, senior citizens' talent contests, exhibitions of local art.

The light glistened on the sleeked black hair of Calridge, leader of the opposition. Gliston, like most of his party, was flecked with badger grey, insignia won in a running battle that had ended in compromise. 'It wearies me; you say it wearies you.' The opposition were fresh and sharp, their ranks ever renewed while his were pared away by simple process of time. Doctors, lawyers, shopkeepers, self-propagating pillars of the community, they sprang up strong and fully armed wherever money was sown. Gliston's boys were old men. Their bright youngsters, once up the educational ladder, moved away leaving aging parents in the industrial cottages, the half-educated in the council flats and the immigrants stacked up in Victorian mansions: all unconcerned as long as the rates didn't go up. Schools, libraries, what the tracts always called amenities were things he struggled for more and more feebly under the trammelling net of their indifference.

The ponderous compassion that weighed like a lump of unkneaded clay in his chest moved out to embrace the whole area. He loved it with a sentimentality that sickened him: the common, the undistinguished fake temple of the Town Hall, the sooty Rhinecastle of the library that overhung the millrace streets; the identity that was so tenuous that what was true of here was also true of almost every other part of the city fringing the central tourist attractions; that had grown up in response to the overnight urban needs of the great population explosion at the end of the nineteenth century. And yet there was a difference, a uniqueness scarcely perceptible to the alien eye. To Gliston this undistinguished piece of ground was singular, unrivalled in its power to twist his heart into a bloody pulp and leave him weak with love. The fly fell back onto the sill with a soft thud and lay with its six black plastic legs beating idly at the air.

Two

'Dear heart, come in. The audience is assembled and now with you the stars begin to arrive.'

'And whom have you cast for the bit parts?' she said, gathering her wit in the recognized convolutions around her, a protective cloak dark as a magician's, spangled with symbols to catch and throw back the sharp glances that might have pierced her illusion and revealed the vulnerable underbelly.

'Oh Henry's doubling up as usual. Barmaid and Boots in one. "Only with you, it's bar none," I said to him, "and anything to get into an apron. But if you're taking to fetichism in your forties we shall have to part."' He took her coat and dumped it on top of the motley pile on the bed. 'Just look at this.' He held up a shaggy orange cape. 'Even King Kong's taken to drag. We've got the prettiest thing in lights you ever saw just joined the company and Henry's persuaded him to show some psychedelic movies. They spent hours in here this afternoon looking for a suitable sheet. I must get you a large drink sweetie, none of that effete fruitcup I give the rest of them to sip at. "Blushful Hippocrene" I've called it this time. Special offer at the local vini: a dozen of Spanish roses. Then I'll introduce you to some of these hideous people.'

He had made her laugh. He steered her past the cluster around the Victorian washstand basin, 'Winking at the brim,' he said, with bloodied slices of fruit, 'Henry's wearing the "beaded bubbles,"' and into the kitchen where he poured half a tumbler of gin, adding a dash of red Cinzano. 'And now no one'll know the difference. You must meet D.B. Hackett. He's eighty if he's a day but a terribly sexy old thing. Never stays

45

beyond the first act; just rings up one of the youngsters of sixty when he thinks it's all over and asks him what the curtain was. Knocks off his piece in half an hour and so to bed. Not that what he does is any worse than any other game of cricket on the hearth. Keep his hands full of glass.'

If he was capable of loving anyone, he thought, as a large white fleshed girl floundered toward him caught in a black net, then he loved her. 'Darling have you anything at all on under that? You knitted it yourself? How terribly clever. It's the dropped stitches that are so in the right place.' As he turned from the fruitcup and dimpled at the enmeshed mermaid he could see her set against the deep-blue velvet curtains in the corner where he had placed her back to an angle of wall and window, and thought if ever there were women who were born to be queens then surely she was and that he couldn't have dressed her better himself with the whole of the wardrobe to play with. Now she was flirting ostentatiously with old Hackett who simpered in delight while two nondescript young men, refugees from a crowd scene and hoping to be paid by the night, threw her a high ball which she flicked back without taking her attention from the old man. Only that moment, suddenly, wincingly, he caught the pain behind her eyes and turned back to his party, plunging both hands up to the elbows in it like a bran tub and coming up with clenched fists empty.

'Christopher,' Henry was calling him. He must organize, direct. The magic must be cast. His hands flowed into conjuring gestures. Life mustn't be allowed to distract him from art. The mermaid was signalling to him again with her empty glass. Vaguely he wondered what had happened to the young man who had brought and abandoned her though he suspected he might stumble over him in the darkened warmth of Henry's study, where so many ill-laid progeny were conceived, locked in the embrace of the A.S.M. who had disappeared too and was supposed to be so good out front. Henry's womb he called the study and sometimes the steam womb after a lisping lad they had once picked up at the Turkish baths in Russell Square and run alternately for a brief week between them, matinees and evening shows about.

'You must all see the lights,' he cried. It would please Henry. 'It's better than Blackpool, and I should know.' He shepherded, cajoled, took the mermaid by a damp hand, drew them after, processing into the dining room where the sheet had been pinned to the picture rail, noticing that she didn't follow, was not to be drawn, but shooed Hackett and the nondescripts to follow him in the dance and was smiling at him ironically over shoulders that pressed forward now beyond his control to hold them back, and murmurs, cries, almost he expected that delicious banging together of hands, rose and slaked his limitless thirst for applause.

Almost he was sickened by how easily they fell for showmanship. In the jungle twilight of the room the snake and the amoeba writhed in blurred tropical plumage up Henry's sheet and slid furrily into the dark wall. The half articulate cries of a pop group ricocheted overhead like parakeets. 'Son et Lumière,' called Henry. 'Isn't he clever?' indicating the tense silhouette at the projector. 'It's all done with oil filters.'

'In my day,' he called back in the dialect of Old High Camp one of Henry's academic friends had described as all 'B' mutations and affronting of back vowels, 'we were manual workers. Automation's taking the pleasure out of traditional crafts. What we need now is Henry to give us fruity renderings from Dorian Gray and we'll have a knighthood in the family. You know you've always wanted to play the Dame. Dancing,' he cried suddenly, feeling the curtain about to come down, the clapping grow spasmodic. 'Why isn't anybody dancing?' and drew the mermaid into the shake or whatever they were calling it this half-year. As long as you could pitch your legs somewhere between the sand dance and the soft-shoe shuffle you were all right and that applied to most activities when you came to think about it. But he mustn't. Not just now anyway. Perhaps later when he saw what was left by the time they were all awash with fruitcup and beginning to drift away. So rarely did the gods throw up anything nice at his own parties.

It was time to begin a little permutation. Someone must be found for the mermaid who would soon be incapable of doing anything for herself and would probably sink gasping to the carpet like a stranded porpoise. There was Leo who liked to have his cake and eat it too. He beckoned frenetically. 'Take her, dear boy. I've played the lovely creature for you and she has caught herself in her own net.' The mermaid giggled and drew a strand of moist seaweed out of her eyes.

'Have you really got a tail?' he heard Leo murmuring as he hurried away. 'What do you do with it while you dance?'

The corner by the window was empty. Looking round he

decided she must be in the kitchen refilling with gin or fled to the 'loo but Henry was calling him again and he loved Henry too.

'When we met,' she said.

  'At the party?'

  'How was it for you?'

  'Don't you know?'

  'I like to hear you say it, and I'm always a little afraid, after something like that, that the other person will say, "No, that wasn't how it happened, that wasn't how I felt at all."'

  'But we know it was,' he said.

  'Yes yes, we do.' She gave the words a sudden fierceness that he knew and loved in her as if they were driven out by a conviction she couldn't suppress. 'I like to remember, to go through and through our love so that no moment is lost.'

  'When you looked at me across that room I was lost then and I have been ever since. I knew but I didn't put a name to it,' he said slowly.

  'Isn't it strange, so strange that it should happen. Did you know? I didn't.'

  'I knew I wanted you. It was like being struck by lightning, as if I lost consciousness in that second and woke a different person.'

  'I wanted you to kiss me.'

  'Did you? You tried to get away but I held on to your hands and wouldn't let you.' He remembered with pride his obstinate strength that had swamped his fear that she might repulse him.

  'Why didn't you kiss me?'

  'I was afraid to.'

  'Did you want to?'

  'Yes.'

  'And then you wrote to me.'

  'What did you think?' It was his turn to ask.

  'I was afraid then.'

  'And when I rang you?'

  'I found a date as far away as I could. That should have shown you.'

  'I didn't understand. I'm not very bright,' he propitiated.

'I thought perhaps I'd misinterpreted; that you didn't want me.'

'But you didn't give up. You tried to make it sooner.'

'I couldn't give up. I will never give up. I will always come and find you, beat my way into you whether it's you or something outside drawing you away.'

'I know,' she said, 'and I lean on that knowledge. You can't imagine how important it is to know that you'll never stop halfway and wonder whether it's worth it.'

'I haven't any choice,' he said. 'I hadn't then and I haven't now.'

'Did you want me that badly?'

'I know I'd never wanted anyone as much.' He laughed. 'All weekend I worried over that letter, whether I'd made a fool of myself by assuming that something had happened that hadn't for you and that when I rang I'd get a smart slap in the face or that I'd expressed myself badly, clumsily, and you'd laugh at me. I was terrified to lift the receiver and then you weren't there and I had to ring again. I thought it was a ruse to put me off and that you were treating it all as a joke, this persistent admirer you'd picked up at a party and now wanted to get rid of as an embarrassment.'

'No it wasn't that. I was so confused. Why was I so dazed?'

'Perhaps because something in you realized how serious it could be.'

'Perhaps.'

'The long time of sweating and waiting so that by the time I came to fetch you that day in the car I was trembling. "Where would you like to go," I'd said and you answered so promptly and so irrelevantly and I looked up the route so many times but it blurred, the names didn't make any sense and I couldn't hold the way in my head. Then I was afraid again of making a fool of myself by getting lost. By then I knew how much I wanted you simply seeing you again.'

'You were so boring darling,' she reached across him for a cigarette, 'on that drive. You talked all about your work and you wouldn't stop.'

'I know! You were very patient. I was trying to play it cool and solid and I was very, very frightened of you.' He had been so conscious of her physical presence beside him that the road had dazzled and swum in front of the bonnet. Wanting to drive crisply partly to impress her, partly because of the upsurge of

49

energy in his body, he had seen nothing of the people or districts they had passed. He was aware only of her body in its sheath of clothing on the other side of the gear lever and his own breath held with the pain of not touching her lest he should startle and lose her. His hands tingled with numbness as they held themselves back and he swore inside his head as his voice ran on keeping its dreadful composure.

If he could see in behind the heavy curtains he could watch them at play. The curtains were blue. He saw them every morning as he came up the path and pushed the heavy roll of *Times* and *Guardian* into the letterbox mouth; blue velvet, a tangible luxury he fingered through the glass. At Christmas when the door had been opened he had seen into the hall while he stood there with his back to the grey wall of the morning dusk, conscious of the dense featurelessness of his own face against the thin light, a negative that would leave no print on the question-marked eyes that looked back at him from the lit interior. He had almost choked on his set piece. 'I am the paper boy,' though he knew it was the custom and therefore the words were without overtones, a simple statement of fact. The bland figure in silk dressing gown had flowed away from him over the gold carpet under the spray of the chandelier to come back with a crisp green note, the most he had collected on his round.

'I'm cold,' the girl complained. 'Why do we have to stand here?' A car drew up, disgorging figures that vanished into the garden and then were thrown into relief by the opening of the door and swallowed out of his sight. Voices, high with uneasy pre-party gaiety, came to him like the sharp hysterical cries of toy dogs and were abruptly cut off by the closing slam of the door.

'I didn't come out with you to watch other people enjoying theirselves.' She shivered. The early summer night was cold and moonless.

'Why did you come then?'

She laughed with a short fierce gulp. 'You're crazy. They all say you're crazy, like all your family. Why can't you be like other people. Enjoy yourself.' He knew she wanted him to put his arm around her, to turn her toward the black swathes of the common and walk hand in hand, his other hand guiding the bike by its neck, feeding her the teasing comments she could cap and return, building the excitement between them. 'Anyway, what's going on in there that's so fascinating? They're square. Old white squares. These English never enjoy themselves like we do.'

'You're English.'

'I'm not. And neither are you. They won't let you be.'

'We were born here.'

'Who cares where you were born. We've got Jew girls at school whose parents have been here for hundreds of years. They're still Jews. They never let you in, these people. You're always immigrants. Damn it to hell. Enjoy yourself and don't bother with them.'

'I want to know what it's like to live like that.'

'Well you never will. It's not so special. We have more fun: bigger cars, real wild parties. Now are we going somewhere? I'm cold. I want a coffee. Let's go up the Caribbean, get some coffee, play the box. Betty and Nina said they'd be there.'

He turned and stared back at the impenetrable windows, imagining voices, a drift of music across the flow of headlit traffic. 'It's getting late. I'll have to go in soon,' she urged again. 'Damn you Alec, you're crazy. Why ask me out? Why should I have to pick a crazy boy? There's plenty others. All right then,' she turned away from him desperately. 'I'm going. Don't bother asking me again.'

He knuckled his spine against the ribbed bark of the tree as she flung herself among the cars, her school skirt swinging against the slim polished legs, her blazer drawn tight by her hands akimbo in her pockets. The door was opening again. They were still arriving.

He had spread the plastic mac for her under a hazel bush, after a lunch in the local pub spent warily edging round each other, the rough horsehair of the common grass holding it up like a tent until she lowered her weight onto it and he felt it bend and give with a sickening pleasure. He stretched himself beside her, leaning first on an elbow and then turning on his stomach to avoid the fixity of those eyes that threatened to drive him to the clumsy gesture that would destroy everything, or so he thought. But if she didn't want him why did she look at him like that? Again and again he dragged himself back from kissing her as they fenced delicately, their eyes holding, burning into each other's as if they would leave only the charred sockets. He tore a long foxtail out of a tussock that reared itself between them and drew it across her cheek in desperation, shadowing the physical gesture he dared not make, a movement so banal it made him laugh inside.

'I thought how corny.'

'It was because I didn't trust myself to touch you.'

The afternoon reeled timelessly, a little wind moving the thin hazel spears, the light seeming to dazzle and unfocus his eyes. Suddenly as if she couldn't hold back from him any longer she had asked, 'And do you intend to be my lover?'

'If madam will have me.'

She had married him because he was different. The other young men hung forward on the edge of their chairs. He sat at the keyboard his fingers stroking the keys with the caress of an accompanist rather than the clawed intensity of a concert pianist, fingers finer than her own, her one defect, or did they count as two, the crooked phalanges of her forefingers so that she always pointed away even when she shook a roguish index at him to keep his eyes on the score and not outstare her as she melted onto her top B. He was older, had travelled the continent. They were such worthy stay-at-homes the local sons. They thought her cruel, a firefly that would scorch them if ever they got a hand to it but that they followed hypnotically from pleasure to pleasure as she sipped and darted away laughing: picnics, Gilbert and Sullivan, church bazaars, triumphant progresses shopping for white gloves and trimmings in the grimy streets until Liverpool was gay Paree and Hetta cocotting with the best.

'Those girls,' her father had cried as she and Meb had chattered and shrieked while they swathed the fruit-flan boaters with tulle for Saturday's trip to New Brighton (she had never gone out without a hat in her life) and taken his sensitivity up to his darkened room until she had tapped on the door with a pretty nothing on a tray for him and she had been his little fairy again.

Meb had been down to visit a month ago in the cold spring

and they had gossiped and giggled until her head had raced and she had had to lie down in the afternoons so that she could be fit for the evening's junketing. They had seen *The Sound of Music* twice and she had bought the record and the score and played it through till it was almost like old times only when she stopped it had made her sad and perhaps that was how she had caught this lingering chill that wouldn't clear up and gave her such a pain in the back.

At New Brighton they strolled beside the dun Mersey waters and watched the big ships coming to port with more money for father and his friends. Hetta twirled her parasol and one of the boys, did Meb remember if it was Jimmy Gilmore, had thrust at her with his tickler. 'How do you remember all that?' Meb had asked, thinking it as sunk in her memory as if under the sludge bed of the river. 'It's as clear as if it was yesterday,' clearer she thought knowing that dun days slipped by immemorable, traceless.

Father had retreated to his room when she announced, pouting, that she was going to marry him whatever anyone said. He excited her with words she didn't understand, was invested always in the aura of the places he had been, the count he had taught to skate on the high frozen lake among peaks and pines while the music waltzed and no one fingered accounts for a living.

She had hoped he would take her with him, that she wouldn't have to prod at life to make it give her what she wanted but would be presented with it in delicious iced sponge fingers on a silver dish, ever replenished so that she could dip and nibble or even stuff them whole into her mouth when no one was looking, and she would never be sick or full up and the dish never empty. One evening they had all been gathered in the drawing-room and she had wanted to sit him down at the piano and begin her flirtation among the staves. Sometimes they dueted; she loved the richness of his baritone that made him seem older than the young tenors who couldn't support her while she soared above them daring them to follow. He waited beneath, keeping perfect time, and then drew her down to him in the final chord. Father had wanted to talk. They were saying something about war, and father that it would never come, trade would suffer too much, they were our cousins and had as much to lose in manufacture as we did though it might even be good for wool and cotton, all the uniforms that'd be needed and Liverpool would make out of that. And suddenly he had said very quietly but firmly that he disagreed, that it was in the very air you breathed over there and that was why he had come home. She felt her heart jump, the lilt go out of the skater's waltz, the star flares die over the blackening ice, a wind stir the flounced skirts as they hurried away. Then she had known she would have him if she could make him ask her because he was different and he would carry her up to that high frozen lake where the lights would go on and she would twirl and sing over the ice while their elegances stood on the rim and applauded.

If only he hadn't been right. They went to the Isle of Man for their honeymoon. Last year she had stood on the Eastbourne shingle on the choir's annual outing and looked out across that noose of water that had bounded her experience wanting to run in under the slap of a turned crest. 'All in together girls, nice fine weather girls.' Hetta turned from the window that showed her only the bleak level of grey-green grass where the wind always blew to the comfort of her room. He was always right, quietly, wryly right. Perhaps it was the disappointment of the war and it only being a hotel in Douglas that had made things not go quite as she had imagined. Not that she'd really known what to expect. She and Meb had giggled in secret over Aunt Milly who'd appeared in hysterics and a long white nightgown on the balcony of her wedding-night hotel room but had gone on to have five children. Alone in bed on that last night at home she'd thought, 'This time tomorrow,' and her heart thundered and the blood rang in her head. What exactly was it that had terrified Aunt Milly? Whatever happened she'd never make a fool of herself like that, however men treated women it was a secret between them.

Had the false glamour of Milly's terror made her expect something fierce that would seize her and thrust her down into reality? Perhaps his very consideration was a mistake. Or was it the childhood surroundings since they had come to Douglas for the summer fortnight as long as she could remember and she almost expected her mother's voice telling her not to track sand across the carpet and to put her bucket and spade tidily under the washstand? 'Nasty, brutish and short,' she remembered from somewhere, though she felt the words had probably been meant for something else. Well it had certainly been short and a bit nasty at first like medicine you had to take and painful, but no brute had leapt out at her and ridden away, and then it had become merely dull and she had learned to pretend to fall asleep quickly while he kissed her cheek and turned his back and the day's conquests carolled in her head.

They had undressed nervously in the borrowed room, afraid of their own and each other's bodies, that they would see their own physical inadequacies reflected in each other's eyes.

'I was afraid you wouldn't like me. I'm not beautiful.'

'I was afraid you wouldn't find me enough.'

'I was so confused by the force of how much I wanted you. I just didn't know what to expect any more.'

'You are beautiful to me, infinitely beautiful.' He moved his hands despairingly at the impossibility of ever explaining to her his concept of beauty, of the limitless satisfaction of the white planes and curves of her body laid on the bed, of a beauty that was fluid and alive like the sea while she admired most the highly wrought, the aesthetically pleasing that left him unstirred.

'That's because you love me and so you don't see me properly. But I'm glad. May your eyes never be opened my darling. May you always keep that sweet madness, that veil you see me through.'

'We were very frightened of each other.' He had tried to make her relax yet had known that all his efforts were only making her more tense and it terrified him that he might fail and she wouldn't give him another chance. It wasn't enough that she should let him make love to her for his pleasure; he wanted her pleasure, the gift of herself. In his fear he knew he was being clumsy and overinsistent. He made love to her ruthlessly, demanding that she should answer him, beating at her until he thought he saw her expression change a little though he couldn't be sure and she flung at him, 'There if that's what you wanted you've got it. I hope you're satisfied.'

Relief and gratitude spurted out of him. As he lay for a moment collapsed on her his mouth searching between ear and throat, his face in the soft hair, he wondered how much she resented him and what had finally made her accept him as her lover.

'I couldn't help it. After all, I wanted you.'

'It makes me feel quite cold to think how I made such a mess of it. But I had to be sure I could, that you would let me.' So that the next time he had been content with his own satisfaction, knowing that he no longer had to prove anything, and that she would let him give her pleasure, rather than force him to take, when she was ready.

Why hadn't he come again? These people all the same, lead you on till you think you there and then and then. But he wasn't like that or at least she couldn't believe it though she told him again and again, 'It's always the same. You think people here are being kind and they are only being polite,' hating herself for saying it, for pushing out the plea toward him, the demand that he would have to answer, meaning, 'You, you. What went wrong? What happened?' Nothing had happened. That was the whole point. When it should have broken into multicoloured flares on the dark, the moment had fizzled damply and gone out and he wouldn't come again.

Retracing that day had become an obsessional pastime. When she got home at night, took off and carefully packed away her uniform in the rubbed-cardboard suitcase under the bed and began her hands on cooking the meal while Stuart told her what his teacher had said and how he could take grade one in the autumn and what mistakes he'd made in his piece, she turned it over and over with the woody yam she peeled and sliced and set to bubble in the pot. English potatoes were cheaper and the boys liked them better, as they would have happily eaten fish and chips every night, but she felt some obligation to the expensive tasteless root thicker than a man's arm that demanded a tribute of spices and flavourings before it would give up its substance in their curry-hot broth. Slave foods: saltback and cheap fibrous native vegetables, pigs' tails and dried fish they had learned to make edible with sauces that broke piquant from every pore till their masters said they stank. Knowing, she had eaten carefully the night before and got up early to wash up and down, scrubbing fiercely at the demerara skin, heating kettles of water after the boys had left for school, rubbing the pale cream of To a Wild Rose body lotion between her breasts, cream in an éclair, drying and dusting, the scented powder giving her body a white bloom, in front of the open

56

oven door where the small blue flames spurted warmth into the sunless kitchen.

The front room struck chill and dank on her warmed body. She would have to light the fire. Reluctantly the paper browned and curled, the sticks smouldered then spat and blazed coldly so that the sullen coal smoked and embered. Twenty minutes with the poker and a sheet of newspaper coaxed a glow that she knew would need constant coddling to keep it in being. The uncertainty fretted her confidence with an insidious corrosion. And then the light went out and wouldn't come back. She remembered again how it had broken her so that when the bell rang and she knew it must be him she couldn't overcome the inertia in her legs to propel herself up the stairs and open the door before the neighbours intercepted. Almost she couldn't bear to open to him. What would she say? So she had climbed slowly and seen the thin legs of the girl on the first floor fingermarked with blue stains like ink, her belly thrust at him and the three-year-old, thumb in mouth, staring up, as she dangled from her mother's hand.

'Who you want?'

'Mrs. Fergus?' she had heard him say.

'Wait there, I'll see if she in. Stay there.' The suspicion and hostility reached out toward him but he was smiling as usual and she stepped forward.

'We have to be careful with this child. She always run out in the road.' The young woman drew back and he grinned down at the little girl who hid her face in her mother's hip. 'You find it then?'

'Oh yes. It's easy.' He followed her down the stairs and she felt the disapproving look aimed at his back bounce off and fall harmless as a rubber ball. Now they would all know why she had screamed at the meter.

The cold squalor of the rooms had startled him.

'I didn't know it was still going on.' His hand took in the ugliness of it all. 'It's so familiar. This is how I grew up. I hoped it was all different now.' Could she believe him or was he saying it just to be kind? She showed him everything: the broken floors, the cracked sink, and then they talked self-consciously in the room with the double bed and the smouldering coals.

'I know you like to drink.' She took a can of beer out of the wardrobe. 'I keep it in here away from the boys.'

'What about you?'

'This for me.' She punctured a rum-flavoured shandy and drank from the tin though she had brought a glass for him. 'It taste better like this,' but she knew that wasn't the reason. Catching sight of her feet she saw that she had forgotten to change her shoes. Down at heel, the uppers gaping, they stared back at her. 'I always wear these in here,' she thrust them into his awareness, 'they more comfortable.'

'What time do you have to be on duty?'

'Oh today is an off day.'

'When do the boys get home?'

'There plenty time. They not come home till four.'

The afternoon stretched full of possibility and warmth like a cat on a sun-stroked sill. She would give him food, English food, and then who could predict.

But he wasn't hungry, picked a little at the cheese salad, forcing himself to munch the cold lettuce leaves and chilled parings of tomato in the dark kitchen.

'Why don't you eat something too?'

'I not hungry. When I'm happy I don't eat.' Alone she consumed chocolates and lemon-cream sandwich biscuits, bread layered thick with strawberry jam, slices of sawdusty Madeira cake sweetly soggy with golden syrup. Too fat, you too fat the mirror cried back at her. 'You don't eat enough,' she said. 'You too thin. You get ill.'

'I can't eat if you don't.'

She perched on the rim of the sink, looking at him and sipping at her tin of shandy. 'You want some tea? I make you some tea. We always drink coffee but I got you some tea.' So she made tea, strong because he said he liked it like that.

'All this drinking; I'll have to find your lavatory.' His straightforwardness pleased her. 'It out there.' She pointed through the window toward the railway track. Pray God no one had been there since her morning inspection. Often the children upstairs forgot to pull the chain or smeared shit on the walls. With fourteen people using it what could you expect. The ancient cistern was overworked and the overflow pipe peed dismally all night so that the floor in winter was slippery with black ice by morning. Fear of what he might find leeched at her momentary happiness.

'That's a dismal hole.' He came back into the kitchen.

'We go in the other room now. It's warmer.' The fire had to be chivvied into a new blaze while she eased him into the sunk

58

and imprisoning armchair whose entrails showed subcutaneously where the leatherette epidermis was worn and slashed. What would they talk about?

'How do the boys feel about their father?'

'Alec hate him. Sometimes I think Stuart miss him, not him but a father. It's hard to be without a man when you got boys. Upstairs they got new curtains for Christmas because the husband shout at the landlord.' It sounded like a plea and she hadn't meant it to be that. 'You like pictures? I show you some photos.'

'Yes, I'd like to see those.' Was he being polite? There was no way she could tell. The tone sounded genuine enough but how could you tell with these people? Their unnerving politeness sucked again at her conviction that he liked her. After all why else was he there? To hide her ambivalent querying she rummaged furiously in the bottom drawer of the chest aware that this thrust the too-tight skirt over the swollen hips into his sight. Some men like them like that. Why should she worry? If he wanted her . . . As she knelt she became aware by the tightening of every muscle in her belly how much she wanted him. Heaving herself up against the bonds of her skirt she carried the thick album across and dumped it in his lap. As the pale fingers opened it she felt the sensation transferred from the cloth covers to her own skin. Would those fingers be cold or warm to the touch? They would make her shiver. She shivered now.

'You'll have to explain them to me.'

Again she knelt, this time beside the armchair, resting her arm on its own thick one sinking onto her haunches so that she was so close to him she could smell the slightly piney skin and wondered whether it was his sweat or some cosmetic, aftershave or talc. 'That is me mother,' her own fingers began to chart their way through the sepia pages pictogrammed in black and white while the tension sang between them and she waited for his hand to move, the touch cold or warm to break the grey afternoon into light.

'And in the end I just couldn't,' he said. 'I suppose I didn't want her enough or something. No it was more than that. It was the shoes that finally did it. It's an awful thing to say but they embodied for me all the reasons why I sat in that chair, deliberately not touching her, not even our fingers brushing as we turned the pages. She was so close and I knew she was waiting for me to move. She knelt beside the chair. Once I dreamt I was in bed with her and she called me her ginger lad.'

'Tell me about the shoes.'

'She hadn't bothered to change them and they were all broken. It made me feel sorry for her. I don't care what people say, pity isn't the same as love. It would have been an insult to offer it. The fact that I noticed them was insult enough in itself. Her skin was very smooth and brown and I wanted to touch her cheek. I realized that I wanted her partly because she was black and that would be just using her.'

'I'd want you to use me if you wanted to.' She kissed his shoulders lightly.

'When people are in love it isn't using. That would have been. I'd have been raising all sorts of hopes that I wasn't prepared to fulfill. Those shoes showed me her need and I couldn't do anything about it. I didn't love her. That was it. In the end I simply didn't love her, not as I did you. I couldn't have held back from you.'

'Poor woman. I know how she must have felt to want you so much and not have you. But you're mine; and you are to stay mine.' Her arms went around him and his tongue sank deep in her mouth.

In those days you could drink the clock round if you knew where to go. He had fallen asleep in the armchair in front of the flickering television screen with the sound turned down, his head propped on a hand, his own rhythmic wheezing a ludicrous lullaby. Like a baby he thought as his mind began to jumble, an elderly baby lulling itself to sleep, and awakened with a start, the elbow slipping on the polished wooden arm snapping the heavy head down on the neck, aware that his feet were cold and that he must get out the long cloth sausage to block the gap at the bottom of the door before winter. It was stuffed with her old stockings.

His father had woken them in the dark, tapping on the door and saying, 'Get your clothes on,' to him and Eric and they had dressed blearily, all fingers and thumbs with their buttons until

Eric thwacked his braces in the dark and they giggled silently, helplessly, then crept out with their boots in their hands while the old man shushed them on the landing not to wake their mother. It would be quite pitch, not even the first pale bar smudged in, four o'clock, perhaps a wind, tunnelling between the sleeping cottages, that had their coat collars turned up and caps peaked forward to keep it out of their eyes or a sooty mizzle making the cobbles shine as they pulled the front door to with a soft click and stepped out under the lamps. He knew how their boots would sound going away up the street. Before they were old enough to be included in the expeditions, he had wakened to the tread of his father below their bedroom window and known the desolation of receding footsteps. Did she know it too or couldn't she hear from their back room? Perhaps she was used to turning over and finding the place empty beside her; no longer even stirred. 'Don't wake your mother,' he would say in ritual and they would suit their gait to his half-roll as if the road pitched underfoot like a deck.

Two miles through the empty streets brought them suddenly into the clamour of the market where the barrows were being trundled into position, the first carts back from the city unloading onto the wet pavements. The naphtha lamps hissed and stank. They pushed through into the low-ceilinged bar that had to be renamed from the Duke of Prussia to the Devonshire Arms when the war came. Father spat the fog out of his throat neatly into the spittoon, braced his foot on the brass rail, chafed his hands into life and demanded three rum and coffees for a starter. Then he looked around. He knew everyone, nodded to them with a quick salute, proud to be out with his boys.

They would drink there with the market people until the other pubs opened at ten, taking time off for breakfast, hot pies from the coffee stall. The old women in their long blacks, foul-mouthed as witches over their glasses of porter, would pat his cheek and give them apples and oranges out of their apron pockets where the coppers jangled and swung making them belly like full udders. They would tell him always to keep his feet well shod, dry and warm and lift the rusty skirts to show their boots. 'You'll see more than an old woman's ankle before you're done.' Without father they would have been afraid of the raw swollen fists of the men, the insinuations of the wrinkled weatherbeaten faces and dark eyes of the old women and the language thick as pipe smoke that flavoured the air.

'Time to be going,' he would say taking his watch out of his pocket. 'Always keep an eye on the chronometer.'

'Off already Sailor?'

'Time for a stretch.'

Blinking in the daylight they would walk sedately. 'Never let anyone see you can't hold your drink and always get yourself here.' But they weren't going home not for hours. The whole day stretched hazily ahead where figures darted and frothed like the bioscope images. Afterwards he would remember nothing in coherence but flashes sudden and distorted as pavement portraits and a babel of comment, anecdote, the Live and Let Live, the Friend in Need, the World Turned Upside Down.

At dinnertime, merry now, they plunged into the steam of the eel and pie shop where they ate basins of salty eels and mashed, gravied with parsley sauce, or sometimes into the faggot shop for slices of silverside, lobster-red in the middle fringed with pearl grey and a ribbon of fat, or spicy meatballs always with an orange dollop of pease pudding. They had been taught to suck all the soft white flesh from the sharp eelbone with strenuous tongue and closed lips and spit the segment, that was like the stays in his mother's corset, neatly into the spoon. Then out into the afternoon to the Telegraph that kept open for the railwaymen, sobering now, reflective, Sailor in the mood for the state of the world and putting it all to rights but quietly, never raising his voice, and so settling in to the evening's serious drinking, the names of the pubs they called at each holding its own associations: the Nightingale, the British Queen, the Cornet of Horse. Sometimes he thought those names and their evocations of the countryside and the past were what had gulled them all into that holocaust where all names lost meaning, became nothing but sounds anonymous as mud, their places usurped by the inanimate whine of shell and bullet, obscene chatter of machine-gun fire, expletives of bursting bombs, the only understandable syntax the patterns of the bombardment, speech a no man's land where proper nouns staggered amnesiac as the shellshocked and only the common were solid enough to hold on to, abstractions flares that highlit and quickly fizzled but would betray you.

It was time to wash and shave. He would have some cheese and watercress, change into his best suit, there was no need to look like a tramp because you were playing potboy, and step out into the evening, leaving the house to wait silently for him. He

62

stacked his few crocks on the draining board. 'Come on,' her voice said. 'Don't bother with that. I'm not spending my life chasing a bit of dust. That'll still be there when we're gone.'

'He was very beautiful and very expert,' she said. 'Unfortunately I wasn't really able to enjoy his expertise. I was too worried. A coffee-coloured baby, although very pretty, is rather more difficult to explain. He was careless too.'

Jealousy turned his blood to vinegar in an instant. 'Was he as good as me?' he demanded childishly, fearful of her honesty that would compel her to tell him the exact truth. But he had to know.

'No one is as perfect a lover as you. You are all my lovers and none of them matter any more. Do you believe me?'

'I'm afraid to because I so much want to. To be your perfect lover is the thing I want most in all the world.'

'Then you have it.'

'You make me whole. You heal all the old wounds.'

'Oh my dear if I could. But you are safe with me. No hurt shall come to you from me.'

'Kiss me,' he said.

The light was dying far out over the course or was it his own eyes glazing under the last round? Jesus but he was a hard man to keep up with that Terence and him having to drive back. Perhaps his own wind and head were going with the late nights and the smoke, the hours on your feet pouring, pulling, topping up and taking a quick drag on your glass to keep you going. Then the mornings of cellar work and paper work, keeping an eye on the stock, the books, the staff. There was that barmaid he'd never forgotten with the false hair who'd slipped the money into her bun whenever she'd a chance at the till until there she was one day with the ten-bob note poking out behind her ear like a curling paper and so indignant when he'd pointed it out.

'What do you fancy for the next?' Terence was asking as they climbed up the wooden stand. A thin perpetual rain fell like a gauze curtain. That was why he couldn't see properly. Why did it always have to rain on his day off? He caught the familiar peat-stack smell of damp tweed, his own suit, that always evoked for him market day and the companion smells of fresh cow dung and horse sweat. And the pigs. He and Brian clung to the metal railings of the pig pens and watched while they had their ears clipped squealing worse than any human in pain and indignation. Then they lay sunk, their snouts pushed into the corners, bloody ears laid flat like aborted bat wings, unwashed rocks jutting out of a shore of filthy trampled litter waiting for the dealers from the bacon factories or, the lucky ones, for a farmer wanting a sow to farrow: a brief reprieve.

Tuesday was market day, *Dies irae* he came to call it later when he understood the term for the pall of terror that lay over the town. It was an animal emotion palpable as smoke that drew him to truant from school and into the square for their doomsday. They came, tumbriled in from the country around, moaning or crying, sometimes silent, rigid, uncomprehending except that it was all unfamiliar away from the known fields and stalls, the routine of pasture, milking or grooming, and their fear spread like a contagion while he felt it growing rank in his own belly. The cattle were the most afraid: the calves run splay-legged out of the carts by neck and tail twisted into a knot, cows whacked into a slithering gallop by the knobbed blackthorns, the bulls goaded shitting with fright into the weighbridge their polished hooves slipping in their own droppings to bring them to their knees while the auctioneer spieled on. But he couldn't keep away, wandered among the hen coops where the fowls brooded messily and the rabbits hunched shivering until he came to the ring of high tense backs that surrounded the horses. He thought the horses were less fearful, more used to handling he supposed, made to trot on a rein, a broken end of rope if a gypsy had him in for sale, or stand breathing heavily while callused hands sampled the taut limbs and prised up the soft lips.

'You're miles away,' Terence jogged him. 'I asked you what you fancied. They're almost ready to start.'

'I was remembering the horses at home.'

'They were some lovely beasts. Real flesh.'

'That's right enough. Real flesh.' He had wanted to touch them but could only peer under a rough-clothed elbow while the men bargained and weighed.

'You don't get horseflesh like that today or men either. By

64

Jesus they were tough. They could drink. I couldn't count the times I've seen me dad worse for liquor. I wish I'd a pound for every time. I'd be the rich man now. Your dad wasn't a drinking man was he? He was more for the politics as I remember though they were most of them dabbling a bit at that time. Look they're under orders. It's time me luck changed. I've had nothing but seconds all day.'

It was over so quickly. One minute they were poised waiting, then the gates were up, a hiccup and away, a flurry of shapes as they took up position and then the final moments of beauty at full stretch, muscles oiling under the polished hides, the flung limbs, nothing held back, the simplicity and self-justification of it against the umbrous olive ground under the rain.

'Dah! A second again. At least this time I had it backed for a place.'

He looked across to where the white letters flagged the winners up on the tote. 'I'll buy this round.'

'You didn't have the winner? At 100–8. You're the cool one. But then you always have been. I'll have a drop of the Paddy to celebrate. There's only another couple of races on the card.'

They pushed their way into the bar that was as cheerless as an aircraft hangar and Tom fought his way up for the drinks while Terence kept a standing space by one of the concrete pillars. 'When we've seen those two off we'll get home to that barmaid of yours; maybe pick up a bite on the way. She's a lovely bit, Maura. I like to watch her, you know. Very patriotic kind of girl. Only likes them from home I've noticed. A drop too full here and there for me but kind. You can tell she's kind, and the way she handles them. None of the old malarkey.'

As they spun home the rain cleared off. 'Does it always bucket down at that course?' Terence asked.

'It's in a hollow. I've never been but it's rained a bit.'

'Like home. I remember learning once at school with the old nuns that the whole of Ireland was a green pudding basin with the mountains round the outside and the bogs in the middle for the gravy. It stuck in me mind.'

'They didn't teach us much, the old sisters.'

'Your dad was a well-read man, an educated man for those times. And a lovely voice.'

He heard his father as the hedges zipped by them unreeling

their new foliage lifting up his voice in the evening as they
walked along the shore and no wind to carry the notes away.

> The pale moon was rising above the green mountain,
> The sun was declining beneath the blue sea,
> When I strayed with my love to the pure crystal fountain
> That stands in the beautiful Vale of Tralee.

As if he had tuned into his thoughts, or was it, Tom wondered,
that he had been humming the song under his breath unknown
even to himself, Terence took up the verse.

> 'Though lovely and fair as the rose of the summer
> Yet 'twas not her beauty alone that won me,
> Oh no 'twas the truth in her eyes ever dawning
> That made me love Mary, the Rose of Tralee.'

Harmonizing on the last note they drew it out the length of
closing time until the inside of the car vibrated with it and the
road seemed to bound under the wheels.

'You'll be getting arrested,' Tom said, as they took a bend
without reducing speed, the car drifting round well on the
wrong side. 'Ease up now. I want to get home in one piece.'

'You're a cautious man for a landlord, a bit of a sobersides.'
Terence rummaged in his pocket for cigarettes and lighter,
keeping his elbows on the steering wheel so he could use both
hands to light up. 'Your dad only drank half what you do but he
was a bold man.'

'I've got a wife and family to support. What good am I to
them unemployed, in the workhouse or the boneyard.' He felt
his feet stamp down on imaginary pedals as if the car was
dual-controlled as they overtook a tractor blocking the lane at a
snail's crawl with rural phlegmaticness.

'Calm down man. I'll get you home safely though she's a
lovely woman your Eileen and I wouldn't mind stepping into
your shoes or into your bed. Aren't we oldest friends? Didn't we
share our last crust when we first came here?'

'Who says you'd be the one to walk away?'

'Ah they always call that the death seat you're in. There's
nothing to hold onto whereas me I've got the wheel if it doesn't
go through me chest.'

'No one,' she said, 'has ever taken me so far out of myself.'

'Sometimes I feel as if I might really die,' and then he laughed. 'You'd find it hard to explain that one.'

'I want you alive, for me.'

'I'll kill any bastard who tries to sort me out man. Little creatures, the finest flower of all the world and they breed them like greenfly and weep when they're slain. "Why won't you make munitions Miss King?" they said to me. And I said, "I'll not do anything that will destroy life." So they put me in the parachute factory. I'm sorry if I'm out of bounds, if I bore you with my talk.'

'Give us a song Kingy,' called a voice from the other end of the bar.

'Young man, do I know you? My name is Miss King, Miss Harriet King. Don't insult me young man.'

'She's had too much,' said Tom. 'Don't serve her any more.'

Looking at his high colour and eyes aswim as if they were weeping Maura wondered if he was really meaning himself. She glanced quickly at the clock as she drew a pint of bitter. Only another half-hour to go and pray God they could all hold up that long. That Terence had brought him back half cut though not showing a touch of liquor himself and they'd both been putting it away steadily ever since they came through the door. She took a stack of glasses from Wilf and began to sluice them quickly.

'I'll give you a hand to dry up.' He picked up a damp tea cloth.

'That's kind of you. We'll be needing all these for the last minute rush.' Suddenly it would be last orders and they'd all come trampling up like pigs to the trough wanting to get their snouts in a final swill as if they hadn't all had enough and more. She looked across at Kingy again. Grey head thrown back the old girl had been provoked to sing at last.

> 'Cowboy, you're a real humdinger,
> You're a hilly billy singer,
> You know how, boy.
> Born to ride the range and love it,
> The silver sky above it, cowboy.'

'Give us a modern one Kingy.'

'That's enough now,' Tom said. Maura looked at him hard. He certainly wasn't himself. He seemed morose and touchy. It wasn't like him to get fractious in drink. Urged on Kingy embarked again on song.

> 'Please release me let me go
> Cos I don't love you any more.'

'I said that was enough.' Tom focused hazily on the small slight figure.

'Sir, should I not sing when I am asked? I am nothing but I have sung before multitudes.'

'If I say no more singing then it's no more singing. Hear me now.'

'And who are you man to say there's to be no more singing?'

'I'm the governor that's what. And you can get out and not come back. I don't need your kind of custom.'

Kingy drew herself up. 'Take it easy Tom,' Terence advised. 'She's an old woman.' The talking had stopped around the bar. Some of the customers looked hard at nothing in their embarrassment, others watched, openly curious.

'Go on, out with you.'

'I'll go, and I'll not come back.' Kingy stooped and picked up her shopping bag. 'Henceforth we meet as strangers. You are a boor man and I'll not drink in your house any more.'

'Out!' Maura had never seen him so angry.

'I am going, but I'll not be pushed by you.' Kingy opened the street door. The bar held its breath.

'Leave her go Tom,' Terence said uneasily but the landlord stepped after her and the eyes fastened like the sucker feet of flies on the panel of door closing them out.

'Last orders please,' Maura cried into the quiet and the eyes drew back to the half-empty glasses, wanting to prolong the moment, an excuse to be sitting there when the door should open again. They began to go up as to a communion rail, holding up their hands for refills. Wilf was drawn in to minister to one end of the bar.

'There's no need for you to follow me man,' Kingy turned back to Tom. He was breathing heavily as he stood barring the lighted doorway. 'I've said I'll not come back.'

'You're a lush, nothing but an old lush. Get along with you.' He stepped forward and pushed at the small bundle that seemed to sway out of his reach until suddenly with all his reeling weight behind it his hand met something solid and it doubled up sprawling in front of him, splaying out, the canvas bag scattering its contents in the gutter.

'Now leave us alone. You're an old scarecrow.'

As if in slow motion the shape gathered and righted itself. He saw the hand at the end of the brown mackintosh arm reach out and close around the neck of one of the milk bottles standing sentinel in a troop at the door, heard the explosion as it hit the wall behind him and the falling scatter of glass shower at his feet. Opening the door he went back into the din of the bar where the eyes swivelled to meet him, torches down a dark road picking him out.

'What happened?' asked Terence.

'The old lush threw a milk bottle at me.'

'We heard it go,' said Maura and then called time, flicking the houselights on and off in a desperate morse code to signal she was drowning under the evening.

One hand holding two dead men Wilf peered out into the dark, half expecting to see the crumpled figure of Kingy flung like litter on the pavement, but the street was empty.

'How did it happen that we came to fit together so perfectly?'

'I don't know. It wasn't there at first but now I don't want to make love with anyone else ever again.'

'And I don't want you to. I want you to be all mine stamped through and through with me.'

'If anything should happen to us, if we should lose this love I should be so sad I couldn't bear it.'

'We could neither of us bear it because there isn't any more than this anywhere in the world and we would know it was no good looking any further, that we'd thrown it away and it wouldn't come again. I love you, totally and only you, and nothing has any value without that.'

'Don't let's lose each other darling. However hard it is let's go on loving at this intensity. Stay close to me.'

'I want us for ever and ever.'

'If we wait for that,' said Gliston, 'it'll be take-over time and too late. 'Course we all know that's just what you're after.' He grinned disarmingly at Calridge who reddened, as Gliston had hoped he would, under the heat of Gliston's knowledge of men and politics. We're not all fools my lad, he thought, watching Calridge quickly arranging his sentences in marching order and opening his mouth to let them sally out but still unsure whether to attack or defend.

'Oh infinitely desirable,' said Calridge, 'but will the rate-payers wear it. They have to foot the bill.' He had decided to be colloquial.

It always sat awkwardly on them, sounded patronizing like using babytalk to that grave toddler his granddaughter. He had only tried it once and been met with immediate though gentle correction. 'Trains Grandpa.'

'Sometimes they don't see the need of things till they've got them and got used to having them. You have to make them have them first and accept them later.'

'Isn't that undemocratic? Paternalism?' Calridge shifted to a salvo of polysyllables that should have had him cowering in the narrow trench of his stunted education, hands over his ears to shut out the meaningless barrage.

'You'd give them only what they want and make damn sure they didn't know what else was going.'

'Surely if people really feel a lack of something they'll go all out to get it. That proves they do want it, that they're ready for it.'

'Coals in the bath,' he heard himself almost spit. Must be careful, must keep a tight hold, only let out the wrath when it would catch them napping and capsize them, blow them all to Kingdom Come. Some half-remembered words jingled in his head.

> 'That is a long way off,
> And time runs on,' he said,
> 'And the night grows rough.'

You couldn't wait for them to want something because the night grew rougher all the while and the vision of a time when they would all want the right things and know what they wanted receded further from him, he sometimes felt, in proportion as he grew older and it became potentially nearer. Somewhere the dream had been analyzed, image and emotion reduced leaving only the bare statements that he and Calridge tossed back and forth across the table, amid abstractions that engendered only a pleasure in conflict for its own sake. 'You teach them what to want with your advertising,' he said. 'Where's the difference?'

'Advertising shows them the possibilities and then leaves them freedom of choice. They can always say no, refuse to buy whatever it is.'

'Then why spend so much money on it if it's so chancy?'

'On the whole people make the wise decision. Offer them something worthwhile and they'll opt for it freely. What you're suggesting is compulsion, the abnegation of personal responsibility.'

It was clever, Gliston had to admit. Suddenly, if he wasn't careful he would find himself advocating a police state or suggesting that people were stupid, easily got at, so that he became Big Brother, he who believed in them, in human perfectibility, who wept inside to see them so codded.

'I'm suggesting that we remove an eyesore to build a public amenity.'

'You want to requisition a piece of land and deprive a man of his livelihood, to put yet another burden on the rates.'

'Ah,' Gliston pounced, 'it's the money then after all is it, not the principle at all? I thought we'd come back to that.'

'And what will you call it,' Calridge said, 'Gliston Park, with half a dozen tea roses and a handkerchief of grass?'

'I thought we might have a bench for me to sit on when I'm too old to totter as far as the Town Hall. There could be a metal plate on it saying: Donated by the Ratepayer's Association.' He grinned again, knowing he had made Calridge careless, edged him into a slip, the tactical error of showing his hand, and then into personal animosity. But didn't that make him as bad as Calridge, his motives as suspect, that he should get such a kick out of his own cleverness and the other's defeat? He tried to lay the balm of being only human to the picked scab of that old wound of why, to keep his euphoria against the depressant self-questioning. There was something to be said for experience after all even against youth and cleverness. There was a trick or two in the old dog yet.

'I move an amendment,' said Calridge.

'You can't,' surprisingly Percy was putting in a word. Please God it wouldn't run to an agenda and give them time to recover. 'Firstly, there's no motion.'

'No,' said Gliston quickly. 'We're a long way from voting yet.

Just a friendly and very preliminary discussion. Putting in the spadework.' He grinned again.

'I want you,' he said. 'I want you again.'
    'Come into me. I want to feel you inside me.'

Christopher and Henry were waving from the doorway. They were almost the last to leave.
    'Goodnight, my children!' called Henry. 'Be good!'
    'Aunt Henrietta,' Leo giggled. At least he wouldn't end up like that.
    'What?' said the mermaid stumbling off the narrow path into the herbaceous border. How drunk was she? He caught her elbow and guided her out of the gate.
    'Just round the corner there ought to be a car; I think that's where I left it.'
    'Are you going to take me home? Whose home? Your home or mine?' Leo hoped she could stand up by herself while he opened the door and got in. He leaned across the passenger seat and pulled on the handle. Back to him she lowered herself into the bucket and swung her legs demurely under the dashboard. She had read that somewhere he decided.
    'Shut the door then.' She swung it to. He would take it easy. Maybe she'd sober up a bit. 'My place I think. You can make us some coffee.'
    'Suppose I don't know what to do in a strange kitchen.'
    'Then I'll have to show you how it's done.' Going down into third he swung the car round the corner away from the common. 'You didn't close that door properly.' He had heard the click of the lock and the rattle as the door and frame drew apart and bounced back again. 'We'll lose you on the next bend.'
    'How do I shut it?' She groped for the handle.
    'Leave it for Christ's sake.' Leo had a quick picture of her opening it too wide and falling out into the road. One hand on the wheel he leaned across feeling the warm slackness of her under his arm, the difference something curious rather than exciting after Colin's hard ribcage, pulled on the handle, opened the door a couple of inches and slammed it back. Swung

sideways by the sharp camber of the road, the nearside of the car hit the kerb, wrenched the wheel in his hand against his strength to hold it and mounted the pavement.

'Look out' she cried and he felt the soft thud as the front struck and the car lift as first front and then back wheels ran over the dark heap on the pavement. 'Oh Christ,' she sobbed and then again, 'Oh Christ!'

Three

'Hallo Dad.'

'Hallo then,' he bent his small head, with the over-large nose that only added to the impression that he was really a tortoise that had somehow mislaid its shell and was walking about in clothing inadequate to guard its vulnerable body, and pecked the flat cheek, feeling his Adam's apple catch on the stiff collar of his hospital visiting shirt as he swallowed. It was too large for the narrow reptilian neck; it bobbed ridiculously as he spoke in his soft rather ponderous way. He was a bit of a guy all things considered. 'I brought you some orange squash cos they said you'd got to drink plenty and I thought it might make the water go down easier. And a few sweets. I didn't know what to bring really but it don't seem right to come empty-handed. You'll let me know if you need anything.'

'If you could put them in the locker for me I can ask the nurse to let me have them when I fancy them. And the bottle on the top. You could make me up some now in that glass. That'd be nice.'

He unscrewed the cap and poured some of the thick yellow syrup into the bottom of the glass, grateful for the chance to be able to do something, best at doing and waiting, and topped it up with water. 'Is that strong enough, enough orange or should I put a bit more?'

'That's fine. I'll have some now. I could just fancy that.' He handed her the glass and she tilted her head and drank, rolling her eyes appreciatively at him in pantomime over the top. Fleetingly he wondered which of them was the patient and at how she sustained him through each nightly visit, except when

77

she was too tired and closed her white lids so that her face merged into the pillow leaving the hair framing nothing like an abandoned wig or the set border to the featureless dummy in the hairdresser's window.

'I saw the surgeon today.'

'Oh yes. How does he say you're going along?'

'He's very pleased with me. He thinks he'll only have to operate once more to lengthen the right leg a bit or was it shorten the left? I can't remember. Perhaps he isn't sure which yet himself but it's to make them more or less the same length.'

She would never know he thought, though perhaps he should tell her when it was all over and those other internal scars began to fade, how at the end of the first week the surgeon had called him outside and said he might have to amputate. 'We'll try to save the other leg, Mr. Rowe,' he had said and he had heard himself answering, 'Take them both off sir, if you have to'; and then, on the way home, staring out of the bus windows at a young woman who ran up and swung herself onto the platform as it drew away, he shrank down into his overcoat sick with the thought of the half-life he had wished on her and the question of whether she would thank him for it.

'I've put the case in the hands of the union solicitors. They've said they'll do it all for us.' This was something he couldn't negotiate, that was outside his province but not his tenacious concern for justice. She had to be paid for all the hours of sweat and pain she had put in that were so much above what could be expected of her, what she or any other human being should be asked to take on as part of the labour of living. Whatever they offered it would be too little; it always was. He was used to that. But if you were patient and quiet they had to pay up in the end. Compensation. He had looked it up in the dictionary once when someone had suggested it was a dirty word and he had to agree there was no making up for, balancing against most evils.

'I reckon we'll all be redundant soon,' he told her. He liked to offer her clippings of news from his day: the only small talk he had since the rest of his life was spent observing in the bar of the Sugarloaf. Perhaps they weren't very interesting to a young girl but they were the best he could do to keep a line open for her to outside the hospital walls. 'Closing down all over the country the works are. Old fashioned you see, people digging lumps of rock out of the earth and us burning it down and purifying the gas and being left with mountains of coke nobody wants any more.'

'What will they do instead?' She'd always seemed to be interested even as a little girl, sitting up all clean at the tea table in her dancing dress come straight from ballet and tap class and questioning him brightly. Then he'd say: 'Show us what you learnt then.' And she'd get down and curtsey and do a little dance for him. He thought how she'd danced at his nephew's wedding and how the guests had clapped. Her mother kept her certificates and prizes on show on the sideboard.

'Oh it's all sea gas now. Some of it's so pure you can feed it straight into the system. They won't need the CO_2 plants or the men to run them. All clean as you'd expect from the bottom of the sea.' The whole trade of gasmaking belonged to the nineteenth century: that lusty child Hercules that played with steam trains and cast-iron bridges, that made toys of steel thought to last forever, that didn't wear out it was true but were merely superseded by the appropriate levities of fibreglass and alloy. 'It's been lying there in a great lake all these millions of years since the world was a kid and now we come along and tap it, run it off like draught beer; all that unused potential.'

At first she had lain quite silent, withdrawn from them, so that he had thought she was unconscious still but it was just that she was too beaten to make the effort to rise to that level of reality where communication was necessary or even possible. 'She's young and strong,' the surgeon had said. 'She should pull through Mr. Rowe.' As he sat there looking at her closed smooth face he was reminded of her as a child in bed fallen asleep before he went up to kiss her goodnight. Pain makes children of us all again. He remembered with sudden and almost shocking clarity how as a boy he had lived a slightly submerged life, as it might be just below the waterline of immediacy until something jerked him into touch, a fish jumping into the warm evening or hooked into blinding sunlight and gasping: his mother looking at herself in the round mirror in the front room; her two dimples when she smiled or when she cried. He had seen too many tears but this child didn't cry, not even the slow wailing of weakness. It was he who on reaching the Sugarloaf on the first Thursday, after his stint by her side, found as he put out a hand to pick up his second pint his small red eyes in their puckered sockets blurring in the smoke and cuffed them dry.

'This room doesn't exist,' she said. 'Nobody lives here. It's just a room for fucking in.'

'Do you mind?'

'No. I'm proud of it.'

Sometime you think these people don't have feelings like ordinary humans at all; feel like rag dolls; don't moan, don't cry just lay there patient til you come up with the syringe.

'Time for you injection,' and you back with the clothes, roll them over, find the unpocked space in the pale flesh and drive that brute needle home. 'Thank you,' they say.

'What you thank me for when I hurt you?'

'Because you're doing something for me so of course I thank you.'

And again you don't know if it's real this thanks or a politeness, a façade with nothing backing it. They born old, so old you're always children to them. When you curse and cry they look at you like you a naughty child. Even over their dead they're silent, put them away quietly in the ground and forget them while we're haunted all our lives, ghosts walk for us, dance limbo in the graveyard, clap hands.

> Back to back and belly to belly
> Don't give a damn done dead already.

Was we always like this or was it the journey that did it, the weeks in the dark wombhold, all heaped together without even room to kick against the prisoning sides and finally dragged out into daylight and a new life; born? Then they never let us grow up, kept us untaught, with no responsibility for our new lives. Couldn't even marry without master's permission; given his name to tack onto your Christian name, like a brand, a species not a person and called Ellie, Willy like a child in school; paid in kind so you shouldn't learn the use of money, buy wisdom, grow up. So you wept and suffered and were rewarded or punished childishly, without reason, only according to rules made autocratically by God and those other gods.

That's why you fall for Brother Jesus who suffered and would listen, who was beaten and wept, who made you at least God's children and promised another life where you would walk like men wearing shoes, not soles of caked red dust to your feet, and long white raiment not rags.

He moved his mouth downward leaving light kisses on breasts and belly, drawing his tongue down in long strokes across her flesh until he reached the mount of Venus with its clothing of crisp hair. Moving her thighs apart he opened the soft outer lips and ran his tongue between them feeling a sudden tremor in her belly as he found the clitoris and probed at it moistly again and again, sometimes flickering the length of the salt wound or questing in the closed entrance. With one hand he caressed her breast, the other held her open while he buried his face between her thighs, inhaling the savour of her, taste and smell.

Her hand tightened in his hair and she half raised herself from the bed drawing him up toward her into her arms. He put his mouth on hers and she took back the flavour of herself from his lips and tongue. 'Oh darling darling,' she said and her face was pale, drained, smudged with the heavy shadows of loving. 'I like to feel you close when you make love to me.'

He began to make love to her again, pleasuring her gently so that she smiled and caught her breath and said, 'You give me such sweetness.'

'Are you going to come for me?'

'Oh yes, yes my lover. I am coming for you,' and he felt her sink and flower under him, opening to his touch like an exotic sea anemone to the liquid penetration of the waves.

They were all children in the twenties and thirties: Gliston doodled a running pinman on his blotter. The things you wanted or decidedly didn't want were so simple, hundreds and thousands in primary colours for immediate consumption and then in the future a pink-and-white marshmallow city you marched steadily toward, your pennies clutched tight in your sticky hand. Then came the war with all sweets rationed, a few comfits doled out on coupons that you had to be content with; and were, belt tightened on a righteous cause that was enough to stomach. And now they were confounded with a multiplicity of choice having forgotten in the lean years what it was that had satisfied them and what they'd aspired to. Now they could pick and choose and had made themselves sick on possibilities and realizations that cloyed without satisfying. They had been brought up without material comfort so that they had come to believe that to have it would be enough in itself and, like faddy children, once offered it, they no longer knew what they wanted.

He pushed his metaphor disconsolately about in his mind while Percy droned into a secondly. Perhaps the young were born older today. It was no good to say that as you settled into middle age you lost your youthful aspirations and that this was right and as it should be. If a thing was right when you were twenty-four it didn't stop being right when you were forty. But supposing it did? Times changed. Well then you looked at it as honestly as you could and anyway the principles remained the same, it was only their application that might alter with conditions. Gliston sighed. He had lost it again, lost even the excitement of embroidering his metaphor in a sludge of generalizations. Groping for something concrete to hold on to he swung his mind back to Percy's meanderings and away again as he felt himself being carried deeper into apathy.

> Bliss was it in that dawn to be alive,
> But to be young was very heaven!

It had all been so simple with fascism and the depression to fight. There was an exultation in it. Even posting manifestos through letterboxes was a blow for freedom. He had knocked his first policeman's helmet off at sixteen in a countermarch against the blackshirts, and the legend of how Churchill had ordered the guns turned on the strikers added danger to the sense of righteousness. Then there was the intellectual ferment of the great debate as the thirties drew to their bloody end: would capitalism join communism to put down Hitler or would international big business hold itself aloof and wait for the pickings when the red carcass was cold? How they had held their breath on the final deliberations, not believing until the very last minute that the English merchants would turn against their Prussian cousins and then the jubilation, the sudden anxiety that it might all be a trick, followed by complete conviction and the rush to join up. Six years he had spent keeping the red flag flying in his corner of the desert, running discussion groups, making sure they knew what it was all about when the moment came for them to put their crosses on the ballot papers.

He had been home in time to watch the landslide as stronghold after stronghold went down and nothing would ever be the same again; the bad old days were gone for good. For a moment he had dallied with the thought of a constituency for himself, perhaps getting in through the union and then the terrifying love affair had taken up again as he walked the known streets and he had thought that this was what he was bound to, would maintain in all its inadequacies, in spite of, or because of, that whatever passion shook him this slow leech at his blood that somehow echoed his own limitations was his love till death did; wedded, that was something he had taken on and had taken him on and he would work for and serve, and he had become a councillor, nibbling away at what he thought were the limitations of growing up and living here according to those same principles, wanting houses fit for those heroes, heroic for him by divine right of birth, schools, libraries, concerts to listen to and ears, and trees to look at out of a window so that no part of it, no inhabitant should be undignified by all that urban life could offer.

He had gone to the great exhibition on the South Bank and walked around exhilarated and aghast at the blending of past and future, that they had done and could do all this, ridden the escalator to the top of the dome seeing evolution unwinding as he mounted and knowing that if they would they could be masters of it all, not blown about like litter, used bus tickets in the gutters at the whim of all those winds of chance and change. But they had betrayed themselves, betrayed him, been codded by comfits after those lean years and the promise of ease when he had wanted them to endeavour and though he had kept his seat on the council the real government had been taken from them. He had almost wept watching the results come upon the television screen and cursed them for their fickleness, their inability to see beyond what their own pocket money would buy. The pendulum had swung again and he had felt the old throat catcher seize him and stop his breath and watched it die away in months of plodding with that old man of the sea economic necessity clinging with his lean tenacious shanks around the neck and his sinewy hands twined irrevocably in their hair until grotesquely the leaden weight of public favour had begun to swing again faster and faster and they were all toppling ridiculous as skittles set up only to be knocked down and immediately replaced. On the morning after the G.L.C. had fallen when he knew that his own seat was safe and he would be mayor with a large vociferous opposition he had gone down to the river and looked into its rank waters that sustained no life and thought how symbolic the scattering of Morrison's ashes in its waves during a sitting of the old council had been. They had been big men Cripps and Bevan, Morrison and Bevin, capable of histrionic gestures of largeness and simplicity, childlike in some ways, Bevin refusing to wear evening dress; politicians yes but sometimes statesmen too, and that last act of the last of them had signified the ending of an era as surely as Prospero's drowning of his books.

Now the age was older, shiftier, more complex he supposed was the cover term to shelter behind. The faces that looked out of the daily papers appeared different in kind or was it his own face he saw reflected in them, his own disillusion? Perhaps the young would rise with a new enthusiasm and sweep them all away. There were signs of a new unrest but it had about it the same smell of violence he remembered from his early days, the stink of his own fear and the animal's as he ran from the reined back and rearing hooves of a police horse, the sweating hysteria of a crowd that fought and howled like children in a street gang charging each other with flying clods and stones and hooting into the November dusks of his childhood.

She lay back against the pillows stormed, swept through, one arm flung back above her head the other resting across her forehead.

'It's all a terrible drag,' pettishly he sulked over his boiled egg, pecking at it with the tip of the spoon, knowing that when he finally stabbed the top off it would be the wrong way up and glutinous ocherous yolk run down the side of his eggcup.

'You know you'll love it when you get there. You always do. All that fuss. Dry sherry in the Principal's room.' Henry swooped vigorously on his bowl of nonfattening cereal like a gull swooping again and again over a heaving sardine shoal.

'How can you be such a gannet first thing in the morning!'

'I like my food.'

'And infuriatingly philosophical.'

'There might be something quite delicious.'

'Oh tempt me do.' Pettishly, the stage directions read again. He indulged himself in a sigh. 'Plump and nasal virgins doing St. Joan. "Don't put your daughter on the stage Mrs. Worthington." "Once more into your breeches dear friends," by Skimbleshanks minimus.'

'Don't be blasphemous with the bard,' Henry responded. 'You know I'm fragile in the mornings. I can't take anything coarse for breakfast.'

'How you can eat that chaff at all!'

'It keeps me slim.'

'An egg isn't fattening.'

'It's the slices of bread and marmalade you pad it out with. You might as well go the whole hog and have it fried with bacon and crisp golden fried bread. You'll have to watch it my boy, you're definitely putting it on and what's more,' he sank his voice to a stage whisper, 'it's beginning to show. It's time whoever it was made an honest girl of you.'

He had dried again. Henry was always so bright in the morning, bathed, dressed and shaved while he slothed in the silk cocoon of his dressing gown, feeling his way into the day like an understudied role. Angrily he resorted to business, thrusting his spoon through the smooth hard cup of the empty eggshell.

'It will do you no good to bugger that poor insensate object so viciously. That won't make a man of you.' Henry gathered himself for an exit. 'When you're done with the budding Thespians and paid your lip service to education you might look in on our branch of the welfare state. The advance notices must go to the printers and we've still nothing between this year's 'O' level set book and *Waiting for Godot*.'

Christopher groaned. 'What crucifixion have I got to endure this time?'

'You know perfectly well it's *Much Ado* because you couldn't face *Macbeth*.'

'Only because you wouldn't let me do it in modern dress.'

'If you'd had your way we'd have been closed for obscenity.'

'It was a stroke of pure genius to set it in the First World War; and so economical: bomb aprons instead of kilts.'

Henry snorted. 'Explain that to the trustees. Madam, we look to see you later and so farewell.' He flourished ironically.

'Oh kiss my arse!' Really he was a little shocked at himself this morning; he wasn't usually so vulgarly brutal.

'No my dear, these days I leave that to the younger men,' and Henry was gone with perfect timing. He had hurt him with his aggressive early-morning petulance. The egg curdled quietly in his stomach. He would probably sit in agonies of indigestion all day, cramped and fidgeting surreptitiously on a rack of canvas and metal tubes beside the Head of the Department of General Studies as the pieces droned on and he waited hopefully for the best of the evils to manifest itself so that he could smile and applaud without too great hypocrisy when it came time for him to hand over the rosebowl or whatever piece of undistinguished silverware was supposed to disguise all the evidence that they were breeding a generation of barbarians whose only concession to the humanities was to intone in the annual drama competition and chorus at the weekly folk concerts.

As soon as he took his place in the row of competitors nervously waiting to be called and snatched a quick glance behind him he recognised the bland figure that had given him the pound, that had paced so mellifluously under the chandelier. He knew there would be no reciprocal recognition of that grey momentary encounter. One face was much like another, particularly if it was black. Perhaps he should announce himself before he began his piece. 'I am the paper boy.' His hands thrust the papers through the letterbox and down onto the mat where those other hands would reach out and pick them up. Sometimes the wad jammed thickly, as the words might stick in his throat when it was his turn to go up, and then he wrestled with it so that it should be out of the rain, the sheets dry and crisp to the touch, until it gave way and slid meekly through into the house. Well, he wouldn't be nervous, not more so than he always was anyway just because he had so often fingered the blue-velvet curtains through the glass. He would be proud and tall as if he was in disguise, a challenger unrecognized.

Sweet shade of Novello! He might have known they'd all pick the same thing. Give them a choice and they'll all plump for the obvious. How many Henrys had he heard exhorting their troops? It was his own fault: he never learned. Six maids had begged him to leave them the larks in the sunshine and the blessed, blessed church bells and two stout sixteen-year-olds had plucked their nipples from his boneless gums.

'Alec Fergus,' the Head of General Studies announced. 'Out, out brief candle,' for a certainty with a name like that. His hand itched for his trouser pocket. Out, out indeed.

> 'My father is deceased. Come, Gaveston,
> And share the kingdom with thy dearest friend.
> Ah, words that make me surfeit with delight.'

Looking up quickly he saw the thin tense figure in blue-denim jeans and jacket and dark roll-necked sweater columning the neat black defiant head. 'I am the paper boy.' No not paper, ebony, wood or perhaps, yes, a mannerist sketch in blue-black ink drawn taut in the page; and the boy could act too, the cockney accent, pared to a minimum by his projection, giving a rough tenderness to the sensuous lines. Christopher sketched in his award-giving speech.

> 'Farewell base stooping to the lordly peers!
> My knee shall bow to none but to the king.'

Then let me be your majesty. I'd have you bow your knees. He must play it very cool but let him know that he'd recognized him, arrange, organize, direct. A note? Or he could be waiting when the papers came in the morning. If he let him see he was recognized would he come or would he take fright? '96%' Christopher wrote on his paper. Top marks. Another Henry leapt into the breach.

'We've met before I think,' he smiled as he handed over the rosebowl while the boy looked back at him with the controlled fierceness that cloaks fear, the arrogance of the shy. 'Perhaps you could come and see me on your halfday; I might have something that would interest you. You do have a halfday?'

'Wednesday.'

'Tomorrow. Good, the sooner the better. You know where I live.' The juvenile lead flashed his most open smile.

'Yes.' There was no trace of an answering flicker. He had played the joke to its full emotional advantage and reduced the boy to monosyllables. But he knew he would come.

'Tomorrow afternoon then.'

Later, flinging open the door of the office where Henry and the A.S.M., and Vera who was their gem on publicity and public relations, sat in conference he paused a moment to gain their full attention and then announced: 'Dear hearts, weep no more; the slot is filled. I bring you a happy issue out of all your afflictions.'

Henry groaned. 'Let the blow fall. My head is bowed and ready.'

'I've had the most splendid idea. A stroke of pure genius. We shall do *Edward II*. After all Gaveston was a foreigner. Why shouldn't we make him black?'

'Can you see the devastation you've caused?' she asked.

He smoothed the soft hair splayed on the pillow. 'Yes. And I'm glad of it.'

The poor girl in the corner bed would never dance again. They had put her in a private ward when she had been brought in and she had spent the first month there until she was well enough for the general ward which was just before Hetta had come in for her check-up. Hetta couldn't decide whether she would have preferred a room to herself. The uniqueness, and the idea of its expense, appealed to her but then she wondered whether she wouldn't have been bored with nothing to look at except the four white walls all day. She was better after all perched on her chintz-draped throne able to shut out her subjects if she wanted to though they'd have thought it a bit odd, haughty even and that wouldn't have done. Never let your audience think you despise them. She had taught herself that when it became clear that after that brilliant opening of her childhood she was to play Cinderella after all and Prince Charming, so clever and distinguished on his gleaming blades high up on the frozen lake, brought down was a self-effacing figure in a bowler hat content to retire into a sardonic bookishness, and that no fairy godmother would work her transformation scene but she must do it herself out of the materials at hand. Mice would remain mice and must be driven out with traps, cats made too many hairs, but rags might become ball gowns, what else but a rag was a remnant picked up for two and eleven-three to make an evening blouse, and six pennorth of assorted trimmings would fashion if not a diadem a garden-party hat for the choir outing.

Hetta had looked at the girl's father on his nightly visit with renewed interest when the ward grapevine gave up the information that he was divorced from the mother who came during the day. She had watched them meet once at the bedside and wondered how they felt behind the politeness, the mutual concern thinly covered by the muttered understatements.

'She seems to be coming along nicely.'

'Yes, they're quite pleased with her.'

'I'll let you know all the doings when the case comes up.'

'She ought to get something but you can never tell.'

Then she had decided he was nice but common and her interest had subsided. He was very neat in his dark visiting suit but he spoke badly, not the words, the words were probably all right, but the way he mumbled over them and swallowed them down only to let them dribble slowly out again with that distortion of vowel and consonant she would never attune her ear to if she lived to be a hundred.

Which she would of course. It was nothing, just a check-up, and already the white medicine was doing her good. But that poor girl would never dance again. Hetta was convinced she had once seen her perform, filling the other half of the bill with her own choir at an old people's concert. You could never tell as the girl's mother had said. She had always envied those who were younger ever since she had looked in the mirror in the very middle of the roaring twenties and whispered, 'I'm thirty, don't tell,' admonishing her own flesh to hold off the wrinkles, her hair to stay chestnut-fresh. That envy had been added to with the years in geometrical progression until at fifty it had broken in a rash of second adolescence now that she could have a lover without risk of pregnancy though she had been careful not to let them guess that as she saw the lights being doused around the lake and felt the wind cut keen through her shrinking skin and the party begin to hurry away. The lone skater remained but he had long since gone off to practise by himself in a far corner, intricate figures for solo performance. Sometimes she caught a glimpse of him as the waltz swirled past and she leaned out on the arm of a young man in immaculate white flannels, caught him poised in a reverse sauté, the eyes smiling kindly sardonic, knowing he had failed her because he couldn't take his times and syncopate them into the beat that would have swept her up before them all to lead the dance. On one turn, her laughter going up into the thin air with the tinkle of breaking glass, she saw that the corner was quite dark and she had lost sight of him completely though she was sure he was still there and she had thought perhaps she should run over and say something to him, especially since there were so few people left, but her own feet hurried her on.

When their turn had been over, apart from the final community singing the choir always led, Hetta had watched the girl dance. 'Light as a breath of air,' said Mrs. Pullinger, 'so pretty too and nice with it, not swollen headed like some would be with that talent.' 'Shush,' she'd answered. 'You'll put her off.' But it wasn't the girl she was thinking of and alone in her flat that evening she'd almost ricked her ankle trying out a few steps, arms afloat as she'd seen them dying across the television screen with a flutter of swan pinions. 'I could have danced like that.'

Now they occupied beds so close she could have called across. What could she say? It would be cruel to point out to her the curled foetus of the old lady in the end cot who rarely woke any more except when they came to feed her but sometimes cried out shrilly in her sleep as if the power to dream still troubled her, and had once even scrambled out of bed in a sudden access of strength and toddled up the ward toward some obsessive destination while the other patients shrilled for nurse who had swept her up in black arms and nannied her back into sleep.

Nor could she comment on those same arms, their strength and surprising softness. Hetta had expected them to be somehow harder, tougher to the touch like the hide of some jungle beast; the dark meat of poultry was always coarser than the light which was why she ate only the breast of a chicken of course as mother had brought her up to do, leaving the drumsticks for the men. Their father had made her and Meb a wooden Noah's ark when they were very small with all the animals in regulation pairs, Mr. and Mrs. Noah who had looked very like the family greengrocer and his wife and their three sons, Shem, Ham and Japhet who were astoundingly all different in colour from each other with only Japhet in the least resembling his pink, russet-cheeked parents. 'As it says in the Bible,' her father had explained, 'which accounts for the different races of the world, the white, the black and the yellow.'

'What about the red Indians?' she had once asked her husband thinking of the stiff ark figures.

'A branch of the yellow left out in the sun,' he had answered tying the neat loop of the statement in his usual deft way that could have made him Prime Minister if only he'd had the drive she packed into her small body and tried again and again to inject into him.

Whether it was that father had found a piece of African hardwood for Ham or whether it was an illusion transferred from eye to hand it had always seemed to Hetta that the black manikin was more resilient, less subject to the mutilations of toyhood than his light-oak brethren. Impaled on a pin spear his ebon flesh showed hardly any trace of the wound when the point was withdrawn whereas the others could be pocked even by a determined fingernail and bear the half-moon cicatrice for weeks.

Lying in bed all day gave her too much time to think. She had always been so active, not allowed thought to take a hold of her in case she should begin to doubt and the whole illusionary structure dissolve leaving her naked on a cold plain of scepticism but when she paused her sharp bird mind would begin to peck at it and, confronted by blackfly at the heart of the knobbly Brussels sprouts, she would ask her husband, 'Do you ever wonder why there are such things.'

'It's part of the chain of life,' he would answer. 'Big fleas have little fleas on their backs to bite 'em.'

'But why?'

'You can't ask why. There isn't a why. They just are.'

'Why did God make them like that?'

'God?'

She had spent her life going to church on Sunday, finding all her social outlets in the choir and the sisterhood. The minister came to see her twice a week. She was a pillar, a tower of strength. 'What would we do without you Mrs. Robson? Shall

91

we say a little prayer?' And they would bow their heads. But Hetta left alone again would say to herself that she didn't believe a word of it. Once she had said to him: 'I have doubts. I don't know what I believe.' The minister had smiled kindly and said: 'I have doubts too. We all doubt at times.'

From the omniscience of her cloudy pillows she watched the comings and goings of the ward, a bespectacled cherub, ready to let fly her arrows at the least hint of romance, blunt shafts of censure, sharp tips of incitement among nurses, patients, doctors, visitors. Even matron wasn't immune. Hetta's bird eye viewed her slight unbending for the distinguished surgeon with disapproval and twanged a fierce glance of reproach at him lest he should respond. After his round they probably connived over sherry in matron's office. Like heroes, half man, half god they should have been above ordinary lusts.

> The sons of God saw the daughters of men that they were fair and they took them wives of all which they chose.

'But how could they,' she had asked her husband, 'if there was only Adam and Eve to start with? Where did they all come from? And what about Cain's wife? Who was she? She must have been his sister and that would be incest.'

'Good heavens,' he'd said, 'why ask me to sort out all that rubbish? If you must believe it take it symbolically.'

Did that mean it wasn't true? He still dazzled her with his long words. She had never lost her admiration for his cleverness, as she would tell people even after he was dead, but his impracticality outweighed it and this was just another example. Either it was true or it wasn't. Somehow she found herself unwilling to let go of those two naked figures of our childhood wandering hand in hand through the enchanted garden, until she came up against Eve being a rib of Adam so how could men and women have the same number of ribs. Why weren't men one short? The idea of 'bone of my bone and flesh of my flesh' dizzied her whenever she looked at a potential lover but it had never happened. Flesh and bone refused resolutely to melt into each other. She kept her separate self. That too seemed a lie.

Now alone on her eminence she decided again that she didn't believe a word of it. As he had said it was all rubbish. Once you had begun to question where did you stop? Heaven, hell, the life everlasting trailed out of the garden in the wake of Adam and Eve. The only truth was the old lady in the corner cot, foetus curled into an unanswerable question mark.

'Do you remember when we bought this bed?' she said.
    'Of course.'
    'How paternal the salesman was.'
    'You were so precise about the size darling.'
    'I think he knew we were lovers.'
    'Who else would have made such a fuss?'
    'An elderly couple with arthritis.'
    'You don't really think you could have got away with that one for a minute. Give me some of that filthy wine.' He tilted the glass and raised her head to drink. 'I love you,' she said, 'and I love our bed. It's our kingdom. Nothing can harm us here. Here we remake ourselves.'
    'I know,' he said. 'I know.'

'Why did God make me with the help of some man and some woman? Why don't you die Kingy?' She looked around the tiny cluttered room. The opaque white television screen gave its indifferent concave smile from the corner. There was nothing on. She had already been through the evening's offerings in the paper. What she liked was something that would transport her: a celluloid travellers' tale with strange flora and fauna and their ways. Then she would sit in her chair and talk to them. 'Dear creatures, you're beautiful! Look at its lovely face!' Monkeys she liked best because they were little and ugly but endearingly pitiful with their child faces and trusting animal eyes. They were never spiteful to each other. Confronted with aggression they conciliated with ape smiles and touchings. A fight to the death was unknown to them, alien to all creatures except us and, she had read, somewhere, our symbol of peace the dove that was, after all, only a pigeon that had got above itself. Once she had seen a programme on orchid hunting and longed for the black-and-white to be transfused with the rainbow. Then she had heard what the native guide had called them: 'Parasitos.' 'You're like some beautiful woman,' she had said to the face of the flower as the camera burrowed deep into it. 'You draw them

93

to hunt you and you're nothing but a parasite.' But flowers couldn't be blamed any more than a dog when it snapped at you. There was no malice in plants nor in the eyes of animals. Man's eyes were different and she spoke differently to him as she watched his comings and goings in the screen dramas. 'She's not worth it, young man, she'll not be true.' or, 'Go after him, he loves you. That's what it's all about.' Sometimes she cried out loud and fierce at the inhumanity and waste.

But there was nothing on tonight. Pulling the battered black case from its home under the bed she took out her guitar, played a few soft chords, and began to sing.

'Maybe you'll think of me
When you are all alone.'

The words were like a self-inflicted wound, the pain of a bitten tongue that stops you from crying out, but as she drew to the end of the song she sang them louder and louder like a defiant sobbing until she came to the last 'maybe' which she let trail soft and high as if she was harmonizing with an unheard singer. There was no solace in the music tonight. She put the instrument back in its case and pushed it under the bed. 'You've been with me all my life, I've carried you everywhere, but there are times when even you can't help Kingy.'

From the window that took up almost the whole of the far wall she stared down into the darkening yard. A lone cat foraged among the collection of galvanized bins, their misshapen lids askew, that sprouted like gross grey fungus at the corner of the row of coal sheds reminding her of the bluets she had gathered as a child and brought home to be fried for breakfast from the autumn morning fields and then refused to eat. 'The fruits of the good earth. You was a silly thing. I didn't mean it mamma.' The cat, black and white powdered with dust, reared delicately on its back legs to peer into a lidless bin. 'Poor thing,' she said, 'poor dusthole fairy.' She had found it, as a kitten mewing in the hedge, had knocked on all the neighbouring doors in search of its owner and then had fed it herself on saucers of milk until one day it had become clear to its hazy little brain that it would never have hearth and home like other cats but must learn to fend for itself and it had vanished to reappear curled up with a torn ear on top of a coal bunker asleep in the sun. At night it howled and spat with the other tile prowlers and Kingy would open the window to hurl a saucepan of water in their direction knowing they would leap away from the spattering drops like lead shot. 'Perhaps I did wrong to try and save you for a life like this. There's too many of everything. Men and women lying together for love and making little creatures they can't feed.' The millions of Asia oppressed her; the claw hands held up over the pot bellies and eyes too blank with hunger even to beg. Again and again she told them, talking to the screen, to the charity appeals in the papers, to groups in bars when they would listen, 'Make love but not babies. It's a marvellous thing to see a little creature running about that's your flesh that you made with some woman you love, even two or three but not five or six.' There had been six of them and they had all been jealous of her because she was the youngest and had pretty hair and teeth. She and brother Bill had shared the same girl friend and in the end the girl had left them both, the triangle fallen apart, and Kingy had never seen her brother again. Or any of them. 'Poor dusthole fairy,' she said again through the window whose glass was veiled on the outside with grime (she was too old now to perch out on a sill suspended backward over the drop, short legs dangling clear of the lino inside) and with the coming twilight.

It wasn't the first time she had been sent to Coventry. That family ostracism had set a pattern. 'They don't believe you Kingy. You're so true. Bastard creatures, they all try to sort me out. Oh mamma, mamma, you told me, "Walk tall!" And I've tried. All my life I've tried.'

'Those who are with me, go out this way and those who are with Miss King go out that way,' the director had said, and they had all stepped up meek as sheep to follow him though they had been her flock five minutes before. 'It may be the war effort, Mr. West,' she had said, 'but 29/6 for forty hours is exploitation.' 'I'll put my work out elsewhere,' he had said, 'and then you'll all be out of a job.' She had looked up at him smiling. 'You can't; it's a government contract. We're directed labour.' They had all let her down, been cowed at the last minute because he was tall with flashes of white distinction at the temples. When she had arrived for work the next morning she had been shown into an echoing shop vast as an engine shed and empty except for a complex network of stays and wires. 'You'll be on this by yourself,' West said. Her meals were brought from the canteen. No *Music While You Work*, girls' voices above the clatter of the bench, no cry of 'Give us a song Kingy.' She had worked alone on the metal web, soldering the sinister lacework that was like the giant pectoral of a dead stone queen. One day West had brought in a letter of congratulation for the work they were doing from the Prime Minister. 'Tell Churchill I don't want admiration I want the money,' she had said.

Turning from the window where she could no longer see the cat which had blended its dusky coat into the grey of fading light she felt the silence of her room as overwhelming as that other had been. For a moment she hesitated in front of the television then she took her coat from the hook behind the door. 'I'm going out,' she said. 'After all, what can he do to me? Only tell me to get out. Walk tall Kingy, walk tall.'

'My child,' she said, 'do you mind if I call you that?'

'No. Sometimes I'm your child and sometimes you're mine. That's how it should be. It's one of the things we do for each other. I like it from you.'

As if he had been born again, raised like Lazarus. He'd often wondered how Lazarus must've felt and at how startled they must all have been to see him walking out of the tomb. Some of them wouldn't have wanted him to return of course, would have had an eye on his job, his house, his wife, been very taken aback at his coming toward them the grave clothes dropping off and that look in his eye that he had been where they hadn't and seen things they never dreamed of in their most apocalyptic nightmare. 'Leave him,' they said, 'he stinks by now.' But he wouldn't be left though he was dead, truly dead, and came back to claim his own.

Not that he'd been married then or Lazarus either from what he could remember. It wasn't much to offer a woman marriage to a ghost, haunter and haunted, but she was very good when he woke in the night muttering and calling out and she would take him in her arms and soothe him. 'There Wilf, there. It's all over.' Perhaps Corporal Lazarus had married too, someone who had watched it all from the fringe of the crowd and stepped forward seeing he didn't know what to do, which way to turn, it all looked so strange, was maybe tempted to run back in and draw the stone to after him, and he had only his own private death to carry about with him or sit quietly with in a corner, not Armageddon, heaven rolled up and those four horsemen loosed: red steed of war, pale death, black famine and white, white pestilence of gangrene, trench foot, dysentery and lice thicker than the plagues of Egypt.

'Let the dead bury the dead.' Well he had tried but like the old saying they wouldn't lie down, not without him it seemed. Or were they trying to live through him? Was it them who wouldn't let him sleep or him who couldn't leave them rest? And now her voice was added, a descant to all the men's voices, clearer, higher, distinct above the whizzbangs, whine and crump of shells, chatter of small arms, the half-submerged human grunts and cries of the ground bass.

'You broke your apprenticeship,' the firm said when he presented himself for work. 'You didn't serve your time and I'm afraid there are no jobs for unskilled men. There are too many of you.' And they shook their heads sadly. He thought he had served his time. 'Done time' perhaps was what they meant. He probably looked like an ex-con, hair shaved to a quarter of an inch all over, gallows clock, back from transportation or the hulks; the sort small boys ran into on the marshes and were terrorized by. His own face in the glass made him laugh and if it hadn't been for the Salvation Army, all gone barmy, waiting at the station when the trains disgorged their scarecrows, with hot tea and de-lousing station and issue of clean clothes he and the other heroes wouldn't have been fit to walk the streets of New Jerusalem.

For that was what it was, wasn't it? That was what they'd been promised: that all tears would be wiped away, he remembered that when he wept himself blind after that whiff of gas near Ypres, and there was to be no more death or sorrow or crying or any more pain. It was a new earth. Four-square the city was and he measured it in feet looking for work, only the pavements were of flint, not gold as he'd remembered they should be, and all the doors he knocked on marble so that he only bruised his knuckles.

He shifted on the wooden seat in reception. They were a long time sending for him but then he'd expected that. A lifetime ago he'd learned to wait, to sit it out. If he was patient eventually one of those figures in white would pause in its purposeful march across the polished floor and say, looking down at the list on its clipboard, 'We're ready for you now Mr. Thomson. Will you come this way?' He would go through that door just over there and take off his clothes and put on a green gown over his sharp ribs and press them up against the plate while the machine hummed and he held his breath so that they could all see the bubblings in his chest, see how they were getting along as they had over the years, the faces of the doctors changing though not their advice, and then tell him not to smoke or do outside dirty work, to eat well and look after himself and he might make a hundred.

A bride adorned for her husband she had worn a big glossy brown straw hat with roses and a neat brown coat. She had always regretted not being married in white, he knew, saying it was a day you remembered all your life like the day you first pushed your baby out in the pram, but he had been glad to match her in his brown suit, earth colours. In the wedding photographs he looked ridiculously young, smoothed down, his hair, grown long, lifted by a Spring wind, as if he was reborn. They had finally given him a job on the railway, outside dirty work but he couldn't be sacked. The millennium was hard for those elect who had survived; not much to choose between Jerusalem the Golden and that whore Babylon for fickleness and draining the last from her lovers who had been willing to die for her but found it almost impossible to live. She had become a drab, a slut draggletailing her dole queues through depression toward a second doomsday when fire consumed the streets. 'We'll take you now Mr. Thomson. Through that door.'

'Will you make love to me?' he said.

'Return of the prodigal,' the flash man said, jerking his head toward the door. Maura lifted her glance, her hands slowing almost imperceptibly in towelling a jug and then on again in swift crescents and set it down foremost in the rank careful that the rim shouldn't let out a nervous clank into the sudden silence of the bar. Should she serve the old thing or not? Tom was still upstairs eating his supper. Kingy's name hadn't been mentioned since that night Maura had christened to herself All

Hell's Eve. He hadn't said she was barred and not to be
served even in the sober morning after when he had been
black overhung as a Good Friday. If he couldn't bring
himself to mention her name he might have filled it with 'the
old bitch' or 'that scarecrow.' Should she interpret his lack of
directive as a forgetting, perhaps a forgiveness? The small
figure was crossing the bar toward her.

'A light ale,' said a voice not Kingy's.

'I thank you man. Your very good health.'

'Cheers. Nice to see you.' Rowe put his change back in his
pocket with a small chink that seemed a signal for talk to
break out again and glasses to be lifted.

'You're looking very well dear.' Maura swabbed the round
puddles from the bar top with firm unhurried sweeps as she
might have wiped tear stains soothingly from a child's face or
washed a grazed knee.

'You're most kind. Will you have a drink with me young
woman?'

'Not just now dear; I've one here hardly touched. But ask
me again later.' If there was a later. It would be wiser not to
be caught drinking with the old thing when Tom came down
but she wouldn't offend her by an outright refusal. What
would he say? The whole bar waited, she felt them almost
holding a collective breath below the surface of words
exchanged, looks given quickly with half eyes on the door he
would come through. Maura prayed they wouldn't all go
quiet again.

The street door swung back against the plum-velvet
curtain that held in the smoke and warmth and she felt rather
than heard the talk hesitate but it was only Wilf, cap pointing
straight ahead as if arrowing his direction toward her. How
quickly would an old campaigner size up this bit of terrain?

'Evening Wilf. You're nice and early.'

'Evening er Maura. Thought I'd stroll along while there
was still a bit of light. Evening.' He nodded at Kingy. So he
had seen.

'Good evening man.'

'Those geranium cuttings you gave me are coming along a
treat.'

'Be kind to the lovely creatures man and they will be kind
to you.'

'Like everything else.' He opened the flap into the bar and

hung up his coat and cap in the passage leading to the stairs and living quarters.

'Can we have some service down this end?' called the flash man, knocking his glass on the bar. She was neglecting him again.

'Will you be patient till I wipe these! Other people like a clean glass if you hang onto your dirty one.'

'I'll finish them,' Wilf took the cloth from her.

'Now what is it you want? A refill?' As she turned toward him she felt the muscles at the back of her neck tighten as if a draught had blown on it in the night setting it stiff by morning. She heard Wilf's voice light, uninflected, dropping into the hush.

'Thought I'd like a little blow so I ambled along early. Just as well cos we're quite busy.'

Taking the flash man's glass she turned to the pumps. 'Would you put another one on in the public Tom,' she said steadily as she drew the engine toward her. 'The mild's nearly out.'

'The mild is it?'

'That's right,' she let the ebony handle go and drew on it again with a couple of short spurts to top up the full measure. 'I was hoping you'd be down soon before it went altogether.' He turned to the bar flap, lifted it, ignoring Kingy's glass of amber pale poised beside, and went out of the saloon toward the cellar door while the voices rose like whipped surf breaking into the silence.

'Soon be Christmas,' the flash man said. 'I'll buy you a gold watch.'

'For long service d'you mean? You'll buy me a bun.' How the time ran on; autumn again. It always made her sad and a little restless and she began to look forward to going home, to the grey drizzled streets and the confined gunmetal Liffey. They all came back for Christmas to her mother's house, except Grainne who was Sister Theophane now and taught the heathen up in Donegal where they ate nothing but potatoes; she who had been the prettiest of them all as if God was content with only the pick of their bunch and the rest of them were the rejects, substandard, slightly imperfect. When she looked at her own face in the glass she saw nothing to please her though something obviously she must have that brought them all running to her, considered dispassionately or even biased against herself as she

100

was. Her other sisters came home bringing their children and they too loved Aunt Maura, clambered all over her, couldn't keep away from her whatever she was doing: sweeping and they were like dust underfoot; cooking and they must roll out flabby grey pastry men and thrust them into the oven with her cakes; shopping they curvetted beside her like small shaggy ponies.

And Diarmid stood and looked at her from the doorway or sat at the kitchen table doodling in the spilled tea with his finger. It was lucky none of them had fancied America; they couldn't have come home for the holidays then and what would their mother have done without the comfort of them all to keep away the sadness of feasts and age. The overhead light fell on his bent head, on the hair that was so much fairer that if it had been hers she wouldn't have needed the bleach. 'What a waste,' they had all said, 'on a boy.' But she had never begrudged him it, only so often her hand had wanted to go out and pat it, know the feel of the crisp rough curls under her fingers.

On Christmas Eve they all went scarved to Mass; her mother's only disappointment in the whole season that Diarmid wouldn't join them, not even hovering outside till the bell for consecration and rushing in to bend an obstinate knee at the elevation as some of the menfolk did. It wasn't quite that he didn't believe he had said when the priest asked him. It was perhaps that he believed too much. 'But the miraculous birth. If you were a married man yourself as you should be by now with children of your own . . . Not still home with your mother though a mother is a wonderful thing and a man only has one of them it's true.'

'Does he now Father? I'm not so sure of that?' Their mother had been very shocked when Father O'Rourke had told her and asked him what he had meant and said she had thought he loved her and was he trying to cast scandal on his dead father's name who had been the quietest homeloving feller any woman could wish for? Diarmid had said that had never been his intention and if blame was to be cast it was his but then he didn't believe in blame and could they have no more of it and leave him in peace. She had seen the tears of incomprehension standing in her mother's eyes as she leaned her red hands on the sink for she wouldn't use the dish mop and detergent Maura had brought her home but kept to the handful of soda out of the jar and the dishcloth, saying there was no scented taste to the crockery that way and a cloth that could be boiled was cleaner. She paid special attention to the Virgin and Child, Maura noticed, lighting candles at the side chapel, wishing to take the emblem of mother and son upon them perhaps and restore the infant communion but he was a big boy now and about his own business, out late every night though sober as an Englishman when he came home and no sign of a girl to marry.

'Who is it this time?' the flash man asked, stung.

'It's nothing to do with you but as a matter of fact I was thinking about me mother.'

Ashamed, shouldn't he be? The cellar steps were very steep. The door had swung to behind him before he could get his hand to the switch and for a few moments he was blinded by the dark as he fumbled and barked his fingers against the rough cast of the wall. It was a good cellar, kept itself at an even 52°, and he was proud of it. Sometimes in spite of the low temperature he sweated down there shifting the heavy barrels and crates by himself. He could do with a cellarman, a young man to help him out instead of Maura and old Wilf who wheezed and choked if he had to pick up anything heavier than a full pint, but you could never trust them, had to be behind them all the time. It was an art keeping a good cellar though with all this new keg stuff and the plastic pipes there was less to it than there used to be. He was always very particular over the pumps, that they should be cleaned out thoroughly every Monday, and he hated anyone else to be interfering with them. So his mornings were spent down there alone in the half-dark, when he was happiest, whistling 'The Rose of Tralee' quietly to himself.

Thursday was delivery day when the great mechanized dray drew up outside, Tom having been out early with a couple of small casks and a plank to reserve a parking space, and the two wooden flaps were thrown back onto the pavement leaving a great hole for walkers to edge by with that weak tingling in the back of the thighs, and the ramp hooked into position so that the draymen could trundle the week's supply down to him looking up from below like a prisoner out of a dungeon.

For a moment he stood there at the top of the steps savouring the chill blackness that was a cold element about him, which he could penetrate or push against and it would give way but flow back again behind his movement, and was held in by the walls of the cellar that he might knock into and bruise himself against, being warm, alive, a hot pea in a frozen pod on a dew early morning, and that he could hold in abeyance a little by snapping down the switch his hand had finally encountered though it would always be there waiting for him when he should put out that light again. Only with the switch he could hold it back. And so he did.

Deliberately but very tenderly she pushed him back on the bed and leaned over him. Taking him in her mouth she began to caress him with her lips, her hair falling across his loins, her tongue darting sharp spasms through him. Slipping a hand under her he cupped it about one of her breasts, the fingers clenching with every movement of her lips. The other hand scored deep weals in her back as he felt himself carried toward a quick, fierce climax and, conscious of his passivity suddenly converted by the rising force in him, he arched himself up, pressing her back and threw his body over her while her arms went round him.

'I love you,' she said. 'I love you.'

He was inside at last. Three times he had circled the common before he had dared pull up at the curb opposite the gate, haul his bike onto the pavement and run it whirring, pedals spinning, up the path to the front door, not daring this time to let his look linger on the enticing blue velvet preserved under glass before he put his hand to the letterbox and then remembered the bell set in the outer rim of the porch and pressed it.

'You're very prompt,' said the voice that played as smooth and light as a xylophone hammer on his vertebrae. 'Why not leave that,' indicating the bike, 'there,' pointing to the bow of the window.

'I'll just lock it.'

'Oh very wise. A terrible world we live in.'

The pale eyes were on him as he wrapped the chain around the frame and through the wheel and pressed home the free leg of the padlock.

'Now come in and have something to loosen up while I explain what it's all about.' And he was walking under the chandelier, across the gold carpet, through the far door into a room that was all light through the big windows, and from the big gilt-framed mirror that took up the chimney breast and from which he turned away, catching sight of himself grotesque in these surroundings and feeling the little confidence ooze out of his shoes to spread a dark stain over the floor.

The boy was very nervous but quite exquisite. He had left him a moment to recover his breath and when he had gone back into the room he was standing in the window backed by the garden, Henry's roses and syringa, appropriate mock-orange blossom, holding the drape of the curtain in a remarkably fine hand; blue-black like a storm cloud or a sulky young demon. Christopher's gut somersaulted deliciously at the thought of pincers and hellfire. He had said he would drink scotch with some water, and gulped at it like a seal at a tossed herring and then again as if Christopher threw his wishes gleaming and arching through the air at him and he must twist his head to catch them jerked on an invisible thread. With any luck he had never drunk scotch before. Carefully he explained his idea and how impressed he had been with the boy's delivery in the festival.

'What made you choose that bit? Most people your age have never heard of it.'

'I saw the film *Dr. Faustus* and then I got the rest of the plays out of the library.'

'What did you think of Faustus as a person?'

'He wanted things he hadn't got very badly and he went after them.'

'Doesn't everyone do that?'

'Most of the things people want aren't worth going after. He wanted real things.'

'And Gaveston?'

'They hated him because he was a foreigner.'

'And will you be an actor?' Christopher parodied.

'I've never thought about it as a job. I don't know if I'd be good enough.'

'You should let me be the judge of that.' Did the boy blush like a damson? 'We'll try some dialogue. You play Gaveston. I'll be all the rest.' Knowing the point would come.

'"I can no longer keep me from my lord."'

'"What, Gaveston, welcome! Kiss my hand, Embrace me

104

Gaveston as I do thee.'" And gods bless the mighty line the boy was on his knees. Or was it the scotch?

'"Why shouldst thou kneel? Knowest thou not who I am? Thy friend, thyself, another Gaveston!"' He had raised him and put his lips to the plum cheek very chastely and then away as if they were miming some elaborate farce. But best perhaps was when he had said, 'Now try the masques speech,' and the boy had filled the room with satyrs, nymphs, and delightful irony on his soft swart lips, his own fair counterpart conjured like another self.

> ' . . . a lovely boy in Diane's shape,
> With hair that gilds the water as it glides
> Crownets of pearl about his naked arms
> And in his sportful hands an olive tree
> To hide those parts which men delight to see.'

Christopher found himself staring at the slight swelling in the tight jeans willing it to tumescence, his eyes stroking the rough blue denim as the boy's fingers had lingered on the rich velvet drape.

Four

'Cambridge,' said Rowe. 'That last sign said Cambridge. We're on the A 12.'

Maura peered out of the misty window, gauzed with their common breath, into the sodium-lit anonymity of the street. On either side the semi-detached, drawn back from the roadway, were moated by lawn and hedge, portcullised by porch and front door, the defenders themselves their keep. 'We're not out of London yet and we've being going for an hour.'

'Slough and the West dear,' called Mrs. May from the front. 'That's where we're off to. I've got a cousin in Bath. Keep on long enough and you can drop right off Land's End.'

'The bar at London Airport, is that it?' Tom asked. 'If it is you buy the first round.'

'Wait and see.' Terence grinned. 'You said fix you a mystery tour and so I have. Now wait and see.'

'Someone should run a book on it. What's favourite? Ten to one on London Airport.' Wilf took out a small notebook and licked the end of his pencil. 'What am I bid?'

'I don't fancy fliers in me drink,' said Maura, settling her fur collar closer about her throat. The coach was warm enough inside but beyond looked bleak as if winter had suddenly gripped it and there were few people about under the sparse lamps.

'I'll take you up for a flip any time,' the man beside her nudged. He wasn't a regular but had contrived to get himself onto the favoured seat and had been paying for it ever since.

'Do you want me black and blue with your great elbow. Sit

109

quiet or I'll go back with the old ladies where I can have some peace.'

'What do you keep in that notebook then?' asked Terence. He had never thought of Wilf as a writing man.

'It's a diary. I put down something every day: the weather, what I do. Where's the first stop? I've never been on such a dry trip.'

'Any time now.' Terence grinned again. 'There's a nice little pub coming up run by a friend of mine.' The coach roared and vibrated along the empty carriageway that sliced through fields draining blackly away beyond the unpaved verges and under fragile spun-concrete flights. The lights were gone. Occasionally another vehicle passed them going in the opposite direction, headlamps, torch bulbs in the distance, blaring into dazzling proximity, dipping, and vanishing, snuffed by the night.

'Where did you get this driver from?' Tom shifted uneasily. 'He's a dour-looking feller for an outing.'

'He comes with the coach. A package deal. He's not very merry surely.' Terence looked across at him as he held the big wheel on course, hardly trimming it at all as the coach ploughed on cutting a wedge-shaped swathe in the dark with its splayed beams. 'Maybe he'll liven up with a drink. We're almost at my friend's place.'

'I don't see how you can tell. It all looks the same to me.'

Suddenly the coach flung itself off the highway, dropping with a clearing of the exhaust into a lower throatier gear, and onto a roundabout. Staring from the windows they saw lights, a half-timbered roadhouse, the Thatched Barn, but the coach didn't stop and they were carried hankering on, up a narrow lane into the black maw of the countryside. 'Here we are,' said Terence, 'first stop but don't get too comfortable. This is just to take the edge off your thirst. The real surprise comes later.' They were slowing down at last, drawing up before a low clapboarded structure, its sign weathered into illegibility. A little dazed, their legs numb with the long sitting, they clambered down onto the gravelled forecourt. 'The drinks are all paid for,' Terence called and with a mock cheer Rowe pushed open the latched door and led them into a bar just above head height with walls earth-brown from years of smoke.

'Good evening ladies and gentlemen,' said the landlord, a small man in dark-blue blazer and regimented tie, with a large

110

moustache. 'Now what will you all have? The house is yours.' Part of the bar was laid with plates of sandwiches, trays of gherkins and pickled onions, crisps, hot sausages in a dish, yellow squares of cheese.

'Looks like Sunday morning gone wild,' Rowe joked. The dart board was opened up, the bar billiards set going. Drinks warmed and cheered them. Only two things marred their enjoyment: one when Mrs. May asked for the piano to be unlocked and was told there was no music licence, the second when Wilf asked where they were.

'That's our little secret,' the landlord laughed and winked at Terence. 'We don't want all and sundry gatecrashing. Coaches by appointment only.'

They drank quickly, two or three rapid rounds to ward off the dark and the dour driver waiting when the door swung to behind them again and they were carried on, the crates of beer stacked beside the old ladies emptying, the windows steaming thick as a bathroom mirror, the songs starting fitfully and high, taken up, ensured against failure by their full strength behind them until no one cared any longer where they were going or where they might end trundling on through the night toward lit city streets.

'What is it we do for each other with love?' she asked. 'This mescalin-taking experience that lights everything from within. Why is it the only effective counter to death. I know that you make me alive, make me want to live so that when the car skids or we're threatened in any way every cell in me, body and soul, says no. There's no small corner anywhere that acquiesces in darkness and destruction.'

Was it the fair she could hear in the distance, an undertow like surf in a seashell, or only a long train channering over the viaduct? She couldn't sleep tonight. They had been around with her white medicine and the Irish nurse had given her a sleeping pill ('Wake up madam and take your sleeping draught,' had been one of her father's jokes) but the little pain seemed to nag at her. Perhaps she would ask for a cup of tea later when nurse had finished writing. She could see her under the blue lamp leaning over the table. The train had rattled them along to the end of the pier and they had sat there in the shelter well wrapped up against the sea breeze that was so bracing it took your breath away and watched the ships pass like grey tacking stitches along the pale horizon and the fishermen pondering over barely visible floats. Then they walked back, Hetta holding onto her hat with one hand in case it should fly away and join the planing, plaintive gulls and to her husband with the other because she was so light herself she too might be blown aloft to become one of those women she had seen in old pictures reclining roseate among the clouds only that she was too well dressed of course and had a trimmer figure.

There had been everything you could ever ask for at the seaside and for a fortnight every year she was entirely happy. After the vigour of their walk they rested in the bandstand while she hummed and tapped her little foot to *Naughty Marietta* or *Floradora*. Sometimes she sent up a request for one of her favourites and the conductor would bow and she would wave while everyone clapped and laughed. Once she sang a solo with them, all those young men in their beautiful blue uniforms, more tasteful than the red, and afterward the conductor made them get to their feet and bow to her, a massed cobalt wave inclining in obeisance as in Joseph's dream in the Bible when the sun and moon and all the stars, or perhaps they were sheaves, bowed down before him, and she curtseyed back. 'Did I get that top A all right?' she whispered to him as soon as she was safe, all panting, in her seat. 'I was so worried about it.'

'There wasn't a note out of place,' he had answered with his little smile.

They went back for lunch to the boarding house and out once more to stroll along the promenade. Sometimes she would run down to the water's edge, scoop up the little ripples and dabble her face in their salt so that sun and wind could dry it to an animated brown. For tea they climbed the cliff gardens admiring the hot salvias and fleshy ice plants; the yellow blotches of stonecrop dabbed into the walls beside the pincushiony sea pink. Up and up they went, Hetta exclaiming over the view from each bend, to the glassed tea lounge. She would have liked an ice but didn't think somehow that hot and cold would mix. The workings of the human stomach, that sack full of a jumbled assortment of highly coloured scraps like mother's pieces bag she had kept for making rag rugs, mystified and shocked her. If there was a God and cleanliness was next to Him He might have devised some more tasteful way of feeding His creatures. It certainly made her careful what she dropped in there, and not too much of anything. After tea they sat on a bench thoughtfully provided by some departed alderman before taking the lift down again to supper. From the bench you could drift away clear out to sea and she would begin her questions, rocking contentedly on the tide. 'Do you ever wonder why there are elephants?'

'No,' he would say, 'because I know they're part of evolution so I don't have to wonder.'

'Oh evolution. Monkeys in the trees. Well you can almost believe it when you look at some people. But it makes my head dizzy.'

'Then don't bother with it.'

'But I like to know. I like a good discussion.'

No one would ever answer her properly. Round and round she went like one of those oxen in the Bible pictures plodding to a water wheel with the walled town in the distance. Below she could see the striped bathing huts lining a curve of the shore.

> Adam and Eve and Pinch me
> Went down to the sea to bathe.
> Adam and Eve were drowned.
> Who do you think was saved?

Pinch me. I'm dreaming. Had she fallen asleep lulled by those far-off waves? Or was it the fairground? In the evening they took the bus under the fairy lights, through the common cockles and candyfloss quarter, to a show, the Pier-rots, or the Minstrels. She liked them best. Knowing they were make-believe, blacking with whitewash grins, Salvation Army tambourines a-jingle, harmless golliwogs, she could enjoy their ambivalence.

The year she was thirty-two she decided to learn to swim. Seven young ministers in training were staying at their boarding house: lads a'leaping, swans a'swimming and all in love with her, adored her in fact but Cyril was her favourite, so fierce in pursuit. Instead of the morning ride along the pier she went down to the beach and they taught her the strokes, upheld her in the water, dived under her, shouted and splashed, carried her beach bag in turn, squabbled over who should spread her towel. When she had had enough they escorted her to the arcade at the pier head where they giggled over the peep shows, not a bit like curates. But it was Cyril who kissed her behind the Punch and Judy show while the raucous puppet voices squabbled like gulls over a piece of carrion and the children squealed with fear. He begged her to go away with him. 'What about the scandal?' she said. He would lose all hope of the ministry. Cyril didn't care. It would all work out. Their church was more tolerant. After all, wasn't it already done in a sense. 'He that looketh on a woman to lust after her. . . . ' He had flushed a little and cast his eyes down and Hetta had caught her breath and felt her bones melting with excitement that perhaps at last that beast might leap out and ride away with her.

That night in their boarding-house bedroom, with hot and cold, she had told her husband and seen the wry smile slip sideways leaving his face naked and young. Then he was on his knees, his arms round her waist blubbering into her lap and begging her not to leave him. And she had only said it for effect, to see what he would say, yet there he was, like a child. As his sobs grew quieter and she smoothed the lank hair she was aware of the last train back from the pier chattering over the frail metal structure constantly eroded by salt waves and limpet life. Or was it the concert party, a door flung open and the sound of applause breaking into the room?

'Don't leave me,' he said, hating the clamour of fear in himself that needed continual reassurance to still it. 'I've never given all of myself to anyone before and it frightens me.'

'The pain of love,' she said, 'is the pain of being alive. It's a perpetual wound.'

'Even when we're happy?'

'Yes. But I wouldn't be without it for a single moment.'

Even here they enjoy theirself sedately. The music blare into nothing, round and round, up and down. No one dance, no one sing only walk about in ones and twos with those blank white faces turning from side to side and the pale eyes taking in, taking in and give nothing out. She would persuade Stuart to go home soon but she had promised him this treat long time before the new school and he seemed to be enjoying it, pull her this way and that toward those monstrous gleaming machines, Molochs that would gobble them up and spit out their crushed bones and bruised flesh at the other end. 'Not for me my dear. You go on then if you want to. Your mother is too old.' They had gambled away a pocket-money fortune on fruit machines of every conceivable design, she knowing that you couldn't win, Stuart ecstatic over every copper-showered return that left him penniless in the end.

Sometimes they passed other faces like their own but they too seemed closed. They get like these English through living amongst them or is it the climate, the skies pressing down or just the knowledge that you is a foreigner, that the intangible limits of the ghetto double you back upon yourself? Not that there were many of them or many people at all. The end of the season had pared the crowds away to a human trickle, sawdust running out of the slit in the rag doll's belly till it sagged and toppled and was boxed up for the winter.

Drawn by the loudest music Stuart dragged her toward the dodgems and up the steep steps to the rim of the brightly lit bowl that smelt of hellfire. 'Take me on Mummy, take me on.'

'What me go on one of those things. You mother can't drive.'

'You don't have to. You just go round and round. The electricity makes it go.' The little cars were whirring and crashing again, the dry odour even sharper and sparks flew from some of them. The soles of her feet tingled with the currents in the metal floor. If Alec had come with them he could have taken Stuart on but he was always out these days acting in some play. Be glad when the term begin again and he safe back in school.

'Please Mummy, please. They're stopping.'

She looked down at his pleading face that was so much more like hers than Cameron's; Alec was like his father: high cheekboned, the thin features carved out where Stuart's were full, soft and moulded; supple-limbed too while Stuart was stocky. 'All right then but you got to drive the bleddy thing.' Embarrassment made her swear as she hoisted her tight skirt and high heels down onto the iron skating rink aware of the stares of the men who were propped against the supporting pillars as if for malign decoration in some satanic ballroom.

Grinning like devils too some of them. 'I too fat, never get into that little thing.' But Stuart had climbed behind the wheel of a yellow car.

'You promised. They'll turn on the electricity.' And then she would be trapped while they whirled about her, or knocked to the floor where her hair would frizzle to ash while they butted her with their blunt rubber noses like buffeting whales. Clambered was the only word for it but somehow she was over the low side and had fitted her hips into the narrow seat.

The music blared again, strident, hurdy-gurdy of popular song and they began to move. 'Mummy, what do I do?'

'Just hold the wheel and turn it a little which way you want to go.' The car spun like a leaf boat caught in an eddy.

'It doesn't work.'

'Don't go so rough, just a little.'

With a bone-juddering crash a red car hit them broadside and lumbered off, a scarlet cockroach with a coffee-bean figure astride that grinned and called across to her, 'You want to get a man, to drive you.'

'Then I don't pick you,' she wanted to shout back but knew it would only be taken as an invitation.

For a moment it seemed as if Stuart had the wheel under control and they shot away but, as she had known it would, the red beetle zoomed after them to thud into their side with a jar that brought her stomach into her mouth and slammed Stuart's head against the cockpit. It was the familiar arrogance that made her eyes brim with rage.

Just because you woman they think they supermen; can treat you like cattle. Cameron had been the same, had carried her off at carnival down to the beach and made love to her in spite of her pleas, telling her it was what she wanted, what she was for, and only married her because of Alec and her father threatening him with a cane knife. 'I going away to England,' he had said.

She had been stubborn. 'Me baby get born there all the same man.' The girls who were born here grew up different, not subservient or fearful, wouldn't take the beatings when they could earn they own livings much as a man. She saw the teenagers arm in arm swinging along, heads up, perky, giving the boys back chat for chat; some of them even wore trousers. They wouldn't get fat like their mothers under their respectable felt hats, bundled in their cheap cotton prints. They were brilliant-plumaged and sharp-tongued as parakeets. 'You think

116

because you slave you can make slave of me,' she had said when Cameron said she was a cold woman. 'You think you beat me with that big stick you so proud of,' and lying under him she had felt nothing but contempt for herself, doubly enslaved, and for him trying so hard to be master.

Once again the red car homed relentlessly upon them, this time head on so that Stuart, seeing it near, sobbed and covered his eyes and she threw one arm around him, drawing his face into her breast, bracing them for the crash. Yet, miraculously their car swung away. A hand had gripped the wheel, the skin grey with engrained oil, the nails underlined thick, each pore picked out in a pencil dot. An attendant clung casually to the back of the yellow bumper.

''Seasy, when you know how. All right kiddo, don't be frightened.'

The ride was coming to an end. She had seen the dark scowl as the red bullet had missed its mark and now she hurried Stuart stumbling, through the avenues of lit stalls toward the gates.

'Isn't that Alec?' he said suddenly.

'No, no. Come on now. It's time you were in bed.'

'There's no anger or hostility or resentment in me anywhere. You are so right for me.'

'And you are for me.'

'Am I? Am I truly?'

'There's never anything you do that isn't perfect: every word, every gesture.'

'Oh my dear you are so generous.'

'It isn't generosity. It's just the truth. *You're* generous. Physically generous with yourself. You let me do whatever I like. You never stop me, tell me to go away or hold yourself back from me.'

'That's because I can't, because I like everything you do.' And then, 'It is so miraculous how much we do like each other. I like to feel you there on top of me, your skin against mine.' She laughed, 'I've never spent so much time in bed with anyone since I was an adolescent.'

Rowe saw it first and began to laugh. Terence winked at him and put a thick forefinger on his lips. The others were still too preoccupied. Were the streets familiar or did they all look the same blurred by the slight October mist? A second time the coach swung off the road, now between high iron gates, under trees, and to a jolting stop. There was a moment's silence. Terence rose in his seat and turned to face them. 'My lords, ladies and gentlemen, companions of *The Sugarloaf*, we have arrived. The mystery tour is over and the surprise parcel unwrapped. What do you see out of your windows? What is more mysterious than your own back yard? What do we live with day by day knowing it is there just down the road and around the corner but passed by in its familiarity? Well I have brought you there. You can have half an hour to sample the amusements, don't spend all your money, then rendezvous in the bar until closing time. Ladies and gentlemen, it's all yours!' Moving to the door he threw it open with a flourish while ironic yet half-admiring applause broke out behind him.

'He makes a lovely speech that Terence,' said Mrs. May as Maura cantilevered her to her feet. 'Where are we dear?'

'We're here.'

'Oh, that's all right then. I always did like a fair.'

One by one they lowered themselves into the damp night and began the walk under the high vaulting of branches that let occasional dark drops of gathered moisture fall heavy on them. In the distance music churned incoherently. Sleep-walkers, they moved slowly toward it, past popcorn stalls, the closed temptation of the grotto, Madame Almira who could tell your future to the top of the long flight of steps that led like a gullet down to the red turnstiles through which the fairground flamed and trumpeted licking out for them under a black crust of sky.

'I've got tickets for everyone,' Terence called back. There was no escape. Once inside they were splintered into small groups, drawn away down different routes, fragmented, lost.

'This way,' said Terence. 'Let's have a crack with the rifles.' *Hit Them Hard*, the notice ordered, *They've No Feelings*.

'Right between the eyes. I'll treat you to a couple of rounds. We'll have two of those.' He picked up the rifle and thrust it into Tom's hands. The cardboard dummies, targets pinned to their heartless chests, swam out of the canvas wall toward them and away again. 'This is better than potting at metal ducks. More realistic like. Imagine they're Black and Tans.'

Who were they? Some of them he recognized: Hitler and his gang though he was hard put to fix the names to the faces, Goering, Goebbels, Himmler, the jutting jaw of Mussolini. But others he wasn't so sure of; unidentifiable caricatures. Were they all dead already or might you be working off your aggressions on the living: the Prime Minister or a famous criminal or just a stock figure: the city gent, the bookie, the hangman? There didn't seem to be any women. No wait. A figure in bonnet and shawl sailed slowly toward him; Old Mother Riley as he remembered but then wasn't she really a man? They didn't shoot women though they had hanged them.

'Come on man. Don't stand gawping there. I've shot me first round.' Old Mother Riley's breast was pitted with small holes.

He had never handled a gun before. Reluctantly he put his elbows on the rest as he had seen others do and laid the cold stock to his cheek. Sights, he had to look for the sights. Here was old Hitler coming around again. There was no harm in taking a pot at him. He squeezed the trigger, clenching himself against the bang and the recoil that bucked his shoulder nearly throwing him off balance. 'Again!' shouted Terence. 'That's it. Now reload and fire!' Obediently he snapped the breach open, pushed home two more pellets, snapped it shut and took up position. 'Fire! fire!' shouted Terence. 'Reload. Fire, fire! We'll make a soldier of you yet my lad. Reload. Fire, fire!'

Somehow he had got out of the house while his mother and sister were listening for noises outside and wouldn't hear his slight scuffle at the back window. He knew they were listening because they always did and if he spoke too loudly before he was sent to bed he would be quickly shushed. They were glad when he could be packed off but tonight he wasn't staying in a house full of women he was going out to find his dad and be with him. The soles of his bare feet were noiseless on the road as he ran through the soft Kerry dark. Up ahead he would be, coming home toward him, and swing him up and carry him aloft on his back in a flying angel all the way to the house. There were torches, pinpricks of light bobbing along ahead. That would be his dad, back from singing at a neighbour's. Almost he could hear the words though it might be his own breath pounding rhythmically in his ears as he ran.

'Dad,' he called. 'Dad!' The torches had stopped. He ran on. Nearly there now.

'Halt,' a voice barked though he could see no figures on the black only the points of light dancing through his haste. 'Halt.'

'Stand still, Thomas.' That was his father's voice. 'Don't come any further. Stand still boy.' But he ran on, and suddenly his father was running toward him out of the lights and the other voice said, 'Fire!' Then his father's figure was face down in the road and he was fleeing back along the way he had come.

'Shot in the back while trying to escape,' the captain had said.

'You have the other round,' he said to Terence. 'I don't want it.'

'Come into me,' she said. 'I want to feel you inside me.'

Would nothing please the boy? Christopher had brought him here hoping to coax a smile, a little delight into those Malaccan features. Heads of such polished containment appeared in studies of African art beside the coloured raffia work and juju masks but they were usually smiling inwardly, ebon male Mona Lisas (though privately he had often had his doubts about the sex of that one and just what she might be smiling at). That kind of smile, that brand of containment he could understand, particularly when it was decked in ostrich feathers and had an Oxbridge accent, camp coffee of the unmistakable essence, but this impenetrable and deadly gravity made him go quite limp. Perhaps what he had thought was pride and wanted to take hold of was only stiff-necked stupidity. Henry had giggled delightedly in the wings at his fear of even touching the boy, when not sanctioned by the script. 'Embrace me Gaveston,' had temporarily become Henry's favourite joke, embellished by sly points about textual glosses, or did he mean glossing over or glozing. Repeatedly Christopher's hand had quivered out, a wavering antenna that picked up the inimical current and fell

120

back. In his narrow bed at night he fantasized the sinewy brown buttocks under his hands, the dark ripe penis, lush jungle fruit.

έγω δε μόνα κατεύδω.
'And I lie in my bed alone.'

Or was it: 'I alone lie in my bed'? No one had ever quite decided. Whichever, the smell of loneliness rose acrid from the page as from his own sperm-wet sheet.

Henry was jealous of course; always was except that time they had had the boy between them, Oberon and Titania bickering over the changeling but closer than in the estrangement of separate involvements. It was almost as though they made love to each other by proxy.

Whereas he wasn't jealous of Henry and the A.S.M. or whoever was sparks for the moment. And Henry's enjoyment of his fumblings or rather lack of them exacerbated his desire for the boy and resentment of his untouchability. He was used to trade of one kind or another, not professional of course; there was no need to resort to that with a continual procession of young actors of variable talent but usually tolerable prettiness, and friends of friends all eager to keep the cold from each other for a season. It had soon become clear that the boy was a virgin of alarming purity, probably a romantic, and of a daunting high seriousness. Innuendoes passed straight over his shoulder to disappear with a very dull thud in the middle distance while the rest tittered and he looked back with never a flicker in the dense jet eyes. Yet Christopher had suspected that the boy might be in love with him. Such fierceness they generated in the scenes between them.

'You can't direct and play Edward,' Henry had objected.

'Then you'll have to get out your tatty old director's seat and be co-pilot. No one else is having this part.' Certainly it gave the play a new impetus having Alec as Gaveston. Christopher's theatrical instinct hadn't deserted him under the onslaught of passion. Was Henry afraid that while unrequited it might become love? Well that danger was over now and as usual it had been better to travel hopefully than to arrive. Not that he felt he had really had the boy; he remained aloof and Christopher had no way at all of penetrating his thoughts. This treat had been intended as some kind of reward. Perhaps too he had wanted to rekindle his own slightly flagging zeal by seeing him in his native habitat, hearing him erupt into that sharp twang

Marlowe had almost modulated out of his voice. And was there too some element in himself of wanting to show off this dark elusive object as his own, to see him laugh against the brash fluorescent backdrop of the screaming metal amusements, lithe and defiant? 'Dear heart you are so primitive.'

'I am the paper boy.'

'You have made me a thing,' was what he wanted to say. 'I don't exist for you as myself. I am only a black boy.' But he knew no way of articulating his despair. Nothing he had learned at school had given him words for this. What was it she had said? 'They're still Jews.' Somewhere there was an echo: 'If you prick us do we not bleed?' what did he want of him now? What was he supposed to do among the coconut shies and chairoplanes?

'We must teach you to cry,' he had said. 'It's a purely mechanical thing, something you learn at drama school. And this scene needs a little extra work. Can you come round this afternoon? We can run through it at home in comfort and the rest of the cast can have some time off.' And he had gone, happy to be inside that house again.

'It's very simple really. You don't have to think about it. Just breathe from the abdomen. Here, give me your hand. Feel, from here. Dear boy, you're very beautiful. Now look what you've done. "Embrace me, Gaveston, as I do thee."' This time he had kissed him full on the mouth, held him close with one arm while he unzipped his jeans. They had stood face to face, pressed against each other, and then gradually as his own climax swelled and broke from him he had become aware of the murmured words, 'you beautiful black beast. Dear boy you're so primitive. Sweet savage, you ravish me.'

And he had groaned, 'I am the paper boy,' and spent himself in ash.

He pushed his way though the loitering groups feeling Christopher hurry to keep up with him but not looking back to see. Ahead a small crowd gathered in front of a sideshow drew him in desperation. As he paused, Christopher breathless behind him, a bell rang, there was laughter and a low cheer. Inside a wire-netting cage a bed hung with mauve silk drapes tilted slowly sideways dropping its occupant to hands and knees on the floor. Smiling she scrambled up, stepped forward a couple of paces shaking her bikinied breasts at the watchers, turned, lowered her briefs to show the shapely pink arse and scrambled back into bed. 'Six balls a bob,' called the showman. Alec took two shillings from his pocket.

The first three balls were wide of the target while he found his range. With the fourth the bell rang. The girl fell smiling at their feet. The crowd applauded. The bell rang a second time and then again. He couldn't miss. The girl gritted her teeth. Impassively he hurled his second shillingsworth; a bull's-eye every time. The young men watching who had laughed at his expertise at first, began to murmur. He put his hand in his pocket and brought out two sixpences.

'You've had your fun mate. Give the lady a rest.'

'Another shillingsworth.'

'Bleeding nigger,' a voice said from the crowd.

'Come away now.' Christopher pulled at his arm.

'I have a right to play. "If I speed well I'll entertain you all."' He laughed. 'Another shillingsworth.'

Reluctantly the showman handed them over. He would miss with the first one. From her violet nest the girl stared angrily at him waiting. He drew back his arm.

'Is that nice?' he said making her smile with the pleasure he gave her.

'Oh Christ it's nice,' she answered arching her body up toward him.

Not a bit like the old Vickers 303. The small boy gunning ferociously for the slit-eyed enemy swung his last burst; the green light failed. The money had run out. Should he have a go, put sixpence in and mock up all those battles long ago? Enfilading fire: cover the enemy's communication trench from two sides and sweep it with cross bursts. Two hundred and forty-two bullets a minute. No one could get through alive. The suicide clubs they called us. 'Wipe out that nest,' from some Jerry brass hat and you died like bees in a smoked hive.

But at least you never saw your dead. The face turned up to the moon as you stood on the firestep looking across the explosion pitted waste of no man's land might have been leeched white by anyone's bullet; the boy held upright by the wire unable to lie easy even in death until they should come along under a white flag and pluck him off like a maggoty apple could be someone else's gallows fruit. No twist of the bayonet in the gut, no butcher's shambles of a flung mills bomb from your own hand that you must occupy.

'Come up with me,' the boy said when it was his turn on lookout. 'I'm scared.' Windy they called him. By the time you'd been up there half an hour with him you were windy too, nerves twitching for every shadow that moved among the craters, eyes straining at every hummock thrown up under the green umbrella of a verey light, its deathly radiance almost beautiful, a bonfire night flame as it fell a slow declining star. And then pitch black. 'I know I'm gonna get killed.' Of course he didn't. That was left to the others. But he died a thousand times before they invalided him home. You wondered why he joined: some bitch of an old regular type of woman egging him on no doubt. Like the day me and Jack and Tosher and others of the lads were skylarking about in the market and Tosher said 'Where shall we go?' The old harridan passing piped up, 'There's a khaki shop round the corner, you'd better go there.' Lads of seventeen they were still and too young to volunteer but you daren't say anything.

Tosher was killed in Belgium but we were a lucky little mob except for Lieutenant Gray and Sergeant Burke who opened their mouths and died. 'Lucky old boy,' they said to me as we stood blind in a row after the gas shells, waiting to be taken to the dressing station. 'Lucky old boy,' and it choked them, reached down their throats and squeezed their lungs to pulp. Then we got Oxo and it was all different.

Mad he was, looking back. Never carried a gun. Must have been twenty to my nineteen; history student at Oxford. Dare-devil kind of a bloke. 'Come on,' he'd say. 'Who's for a spot of listening post tonight?' Leave everything behind that might identify you, take your cutters, over the firestep and through the wire. Then lay out like dead to see if you'd been spotted. A touch on the arm, a nod and you crawled away after him. Like hide and seek only everyone was hiding and seeking together with every chance you might meet a raiding party of theirs, and you unarmed, creeping as silent toward you or be shot at by your own blokes in the dark. But we would have followed him anywhere. So close we were to them sometimes you could hear them cough or the scrape of a match. Oxo'd sign to us to lie still and we'd hold our breath while he listened. He must've spoke a bit of their language cos you'd feel him smiling in the dark over their gutturals and when he'd got what he wanted he'd touch my hand and I'd touch the next bloke's in relay and we'd creep back.

When we got to the hospital after the gas they did us each up in a lint bag smeared with ointment and bandaged our doings so they wouldn't drop off. Cans of Friars balsam you breathed in for your lungs; blind for a week and the skin peeling off you. Then, when we were a bit better, there were all the blokes on crutches from the orthopaedic we could watch going up the hill to the knocking shop in Rue de St Paul. Only we didn't feel like it. And I lay there thinking of that dolly bag I'd got hold of that wasn't mine with a pay book in it with ten francs to come, and how I'd spend it.

Another small boy had taken over the controls and was banging away for dear life. Around him the rifles cracked from the ranges, the roller coaster screamed and whined like a laid-down barrage, the dusty walks were churned into mud. He wrenched his mind away. He wouldn't think of that four days' drowning while they fought to get him out and Oxo fed him like a bird nourishing her young, poking the gobbets into his mouth. It wasn't that. Not just that anyway. It was that it became a way of life, or a way of death, sharper, fiercer, painted in red and sludge and black thicker than purple or gold like the murals in a ruined church he had seen just outside Namur, the half-open shell caught by the falling sun; that daily dying wilder than any loving, and warmed by the flicker of half-jokes, shared comforters and terrors in the burrows of the dugouts; flaring with its own satanic radiance and then pitch-black until the next shot star for four years, and then the return to the grey, the half-light with his head full of voices like the remembered words of love.

'Cry for me, cry for me.'

'I will cry for you my darling because you make me.'

'Oh fuck you, fuck you,' he said and closed his mouth over hers so that they cried into each other, the same breaking wave storming through them. 'Hold me darling.' And she tightened

125

her arms around him so that their sweat ran between them binding their flesh together.

'What's that then?' said Rowe.

'Looks like a punch-up or somebody with a good line in the patter.' Terence laughed and dug his hand deep in his raincoat. 'It'll be time to go over to the bar in a minute but we might as well see what this is first.'

'I need a drink,' said Tom suddenly. Rowe looked at him questioning whether he hadn't had enough already. He had picked the two of them up by the rifle range; Terence thrusting a rifle at Tom and Tom refusing it almost as if they were scrapping though he couldn't see what it was over. Maybe they didn't know themselves. Rowe had taken the gun himself out of curiosity. In a reserved occupation in 1939 the possibility of going to war had never arisen and he had been glad, content to think that it was enough for him to do what he had always done with the addition of a little fire watching. As he had taken the weapon from Tom he had wondered if he was really a bit of a coward that he so little wanted there to be a living thing on the receiving end of any missile of his. Rowe the peacemaker, the perfect shop steward. He was soft he supposed. Even that drunken bugger he only wanted to pay in money. 'I'll kill him if I get my hands on him!' Eva had said in the first moment of shock when they had met at the bedside and it had seemed that the girl mightn't live. But he could only shake his head finding no echo of agreement in himself however deep he probed. Perhaps he wasn't quite a man. The aggression in others came to him as strong as a gas leak. In Terence it was sharp with sheer devilment; in Tom it bubbled muddily, a volcanic swamp.

'You can have a drink in a minute,' Terence said, leading them to the fringe of the small crowd. Rowe had handed the rifle back to him with a 'Show us how you fire it then,' and Terence had shot it off, expertly and happily, taking the gently revolving figure of the bookie as his target. 'I used to go after rabbits when I was a lad. These days I'm more for the little birds.'

'Any price on the second shelf sir,' the stall holder had said. Terence picked up a china cat with jewelled green eyes and outstared it a moment.

'Now what will I do with that?'

'Keep it,' Rowe had answered aware that Tom had no words to offer. 'You never know when you might find a good home for it.'

'It's a malevolent-looking beast. Come on then Kitty, into me pocket and keep your claws out of me.'

There had been nights fire watching, he remembered as he craned to see between the heads of the crowd, when the whole city had seemed to blaze and roar like this fair and he had thought that to be sitting with a stirrup pump and a bucket of water stewarding the works during a raid was tantamount to watching over an arsenal with your mouth full of spit. Somewhere in front an alarm bell rang. The crowd muttered. If someone won something it should have been applause. There was a few moments' silence while his reptilian neck wove backward and forward. It was a curse being so short.

The bell rang again. The heads immediately in front of him parted as a well-dressed man pushed his way back from the stall.

'Will you look at that,' exclaimed Terence. Peering through the gap made by the man's hasty passage Rowe was able at last to get a glimpse of the sideshow. A young woman, dressed in next to nothing, was standing inside a wire-netting cage shouting and pointing at a young Negro who stood impassively holding a ball in his hand poised for the next throw. The crowd catcalled now, surging a little in its anger.

'They're turning nasty,' said Terence. 'They'll have the hide off him.'

'Someone wants to stop the little bastard. Too bloody clever! Treating the poor girl like that. Where's the men among you? I'll stop him.' Tom began to push his way through the jammed mass of watchers.

'Hold him. Get hold of his coat.' Rowe said. 'He's had too many. He doesn't know what he's doing.' From afar off he heard a saying of his childhood. 'If a man uses his fists he's lost his argument.'

'Come back.' Terence reached out a long arm and took Tom by the shoulder. 'Do you want to cause a riot? Let the man deal with him.'

And looking between the heads again Rowe could see that that was exactly what was happening. The showman had snatched the ball from the boy's hand and was waving him away. He couldn't hear the words but suddenly the crowd let out a great hooting roar and the boy shrank as if he had been hit, cowering, then turned and ran off diagonally, the people falling back in front of him though they were still shouting, the sounds tangible as flung stones driving him away.

'Am I too heavy for you?'
  'I like it.'
'Come into my arms and stay very close to me.'

Outing nights were always dismal with the bar half empty but she preferred to stay behind. Hours of rattling about in a coach had never been Kingy's idea of amusement even when she knew all the travellers and might be called on for a song. It seemed the flash man hadn't wanted to go either or perhaps he hadn't been asked. Obviously he missed Maura and was hoping they might all be back before closing time. Meanwhile he was making do with Eileen, Tom's wife who always took over on these occasions with the help of Maura's predecessor now married and living in a council flat with her brood of toddlers. Released for an evening while her husband babysat for the sake of the extra money she made the most of her freedom, took all the drinks offered, was merrier with the clientèle than she had ever been when it was her nightly duty. 'What is love, what is truth, what is money?' Kingy said aloud into the subdued lights and voices of the bar.

'There you are,' said the flash man. 'Why aren't you on the outing?'

'I prefer to drink my beer still.'

'Have one with me,' the flash man invited. It was etiquette; he owed her one and so she accepted. 'And what's the answer?' he said when Eileen had served them.

'That, man, is the riddle; not of the sphinx, I'll not claim that. But no one has ever answered it for me.'

'The only one I know anything about is money.'

'Then you know a little about truth if you admit that.'

He laughed and lifted his glass. She was a funny old thing. Half the time you couldn't be sure what she was on about. Besides there were things he wanted to ask. 'Quiet tonight.'

'Do you miss her man?'

'Miss? Who?'

'Our handsome young woman behind the bar.'

'Maura?'

'A kind creature sir.'

'Not to me,' he sighed. He leaned closer. 'Is it true you like women?'

'Are we not all human creatures? Why should I not like them all when I find them true, men and women? What does that prove?'

'You know what I mean.'

'Sir, I am old and I am ugly; what should I say to any young thing? Now I'm content to look.'

'But women?'

'Am I not a woman? Why should you want to know all about me? What right does that extra piece of flesh give you?'

He didn't want to anger her. Obviously she hadn't had enough to drink yet. He would be patient. Sadler and some of the boys would be in later. By the time they'd all bought a round apiece they'd see if her tongue was any looser.

Why did they all try to sort her out? She had never liked Sadler and she was a little fearful of him inside. For a while she talked to Tom's wife Eileen, overhearing the men's conversation of horses and deals. Then Eileen moved away to serve and the relief barmaid was called into service.

'And one for the lady,' said the flash man. 'What'll you have?'

'You are most kind,' Kingy bowed. 'I'll have a scotch.' The beer was beginning to swill about in her stomach. She couldn't refuse. It was etiquette. The next round was Sadler's. By now they had entangled her in their talk. Sadler seemingly had a garden and wanted her advice on pruning his roses, listening very seriously as she gave it, his small head cocked like an alert ferret.

Kingy bought the next round. They tried to dissuade her but she insisted. It was etiquette. If you drank with men then you paid your shout or you were nothing but a barfly and could be expected to pay in kind or get the reputation of a scrounger and lose all dignity, all right to be treated with respect. What is truth, what is money?

'What is love?' asked the flash man.

'Love is when two people look and they just know.'

'Man and woman?'

'Or man and man or woman and woman. It's all the same.'

'Not to me,' the flash man laughed.

'So you can do what you like?' said Sadler.

'As long as you don't make babies, bring more little creatures into the world when we can't feed the ones we've got.'

'You don't think about that in the heat of the moment.'

'No man, and that's where men are filth if you'll pardon me. They don't think. Kiss her, make love to her. Kisses leave no scars. But be careful.'

Maura's stand-in rang the bell for last orders. 'We're going back to Sadler's,' said the flash man. 'Why don't you come with us. It's a shame to break the party up.'

'And be the only female there?'

'No,' Sadler put in quickly. 'There'll be my wife.'

'You're not afraid?' said the flash man.

'Afraid!' Kingy picked up her bag. The men were buying quarts of beer to take away. 'I'll have a bottle of scotch, Eileen please. "Walk tall Kingy", my mother always said to me. Little as I am I'll not be afraid for any man.'

'We have so many modes of loving, of making love, my darling. Sometimes I think we are all the lovers in the world, in all times and all places.'

She had seen him run off or rather not run but thrust himself stiff-legged at the crowd and an echo somewhere in him of a gesture as they fell back, though what it was she couldn't quite pin down, what aboriginal cry ricocheted silently from the split damson of his mouth, started her after him, her own stout legs moving as if of themselves. Or could it just be the drink? Someone, was it that Terence, had produced a bottle of gin from the coach and persuaded her to more than her fair share. Maura could see them on the other side of the press, had seen Tom fighting his way forward and then dragged back as though jerked on a rope end, puppet or unbroken horse, but she hadn't time for any more or she would lose the slight dark figure that was sharp as a noon shadow but as easily swallowed by the encroaching night. Following behind him she saw for a

130

subliminal second the rendezvous bar beaconing its neon flush and then they were heading away from the lights, past the tree walk where fantasy insects, given a Disney acceptability, humped their plastic segments and spread spun-celluloid wings, and the cascade steps blooming with drowned flares spurted their milky ejaculations against a black screen, on into the parkland.

There must be other couples there if she could see them in the dark, glowworming in love. But perhaps you could only hear them. It was better to think the faint rustlings were courting, then you weren't afraid. Where had he gone? She had lost sight of him a bit. Then a burst of music, the dodgems were starting up again, and an apprehension of light, not perhaps the real thing but only her eyes accustoming themselves to this more nocturnal circle, gave him back to her against the trunk of a tree, crenelating its own straight silhouette with the indentations of his profile like the battlements of Dublin castle only vertical. She had had too much of that gin.

He was spewing painfully on an empty stomach maybe sluiced with unaccustomed drink though it might be only the fright or misery making him heave his guts into the earth and cling to the tree for support. But it was the dry contractions she heard, like sobbing, that made her step forward. 'That's enough now. There's nothing left in you but your soul and that you can't throw out.' She knew he was too weak to run further.

'Leave me alone.'

'It's all right. I won't bite you.'

Wearily now he leaned against the tree and she was aware that this time they were simple tears that flowed out of him. 'Why don't you go on home?'

'I can't. I can't.'

'Well you can't stay here.' Maura looked around at the cold park. Who knew what he might do if she left him; run away very likely and his mother never see him again. 'Come on, come back with me. I'll make you a cup of tea or coffee if you'd rather. It's not far. Then when you've pulled yourself together a bit you can go on home.' She put out a hand and touched his arm and though he flinched away she knew he would follow, that there are times when however much you may say no and leave me alone what you really want is just the opposite. 'Come on now.' She moved away a few steps and then turned. 'Come on.' The figure detached itself lingeringly from the tree trunk like a black paper cutout and shadowed her between the bushes and onto the road. Should she be afraid? But he was only a bit of a kid. Even when they reached the lit streets he made no attempt to catch her up but she knew he was still there, his footsteps on the pavement trailing her to the gate and up the path as she put her key in the lock and led him through the hall and down to her flat.

'I live in a basement,' he said. 'But it isn't like this.' They were the first words he had offered her of himself.

'I do me best with it,' she said to hide her pride. 'Just because it's a basement there's no reason why it can't be a home too. Would you rather have tea or coffee?'

'Tea, please.'

Quickly she snatched a look at him. 'If you'd like a bit of a wash while I make it, it's through that door.'

'Thanks,' he ducked away out of sight.

'Sugar?'

'Two please.' He was surely a polite boy.

'What was it all about back there?'

He shook his head. How could he explain: I loved him, I was Gaveston and he made me a thing? For a time he had had another being, time and place; had inhabited a court hung with blue velvet, gone dressed in silk. The dream persisted even at home and walking on the enamelled green-and-gold common. His morning ride to the theatre, arched over the dropped handlebars, was a progress. In a moment, with a dozen words, the features behind the grease paint had sagged, the lines etched themselves in wearily. His very flesh felt torn and crumpled. 'I am the paper boy.'

'What did you say?'

Again he shook his head, unable to speak. In panic he realized he was going to cry, that the unspoken words had knotted in his throat, and struggled to his feet out of the armchair looking wildly for somewhere to set his cup and saucer.

'What is it? What's the matter?'

The answer rose inexorably and choked him. Clenching his fists he walked to the curtained window so that she shouldn't see his face. As he fought himself for control he felt hands on his shoulders turning him and bending his head to rest on the plump upper arm.

'There, there.' Maura led him toward the bed. He was only a

child after all. 'Come here to me.' She lay down and held out her arms to him. His hair under her fingers was very soft where she had expected it to be harsh. Not a bit like Diarmid's though somehow it reminded her of his. Why should she be thinking of him now? With one hand she began to undo the buttons on his shirt. 'Here, you'll be better with this loosed. Cry if you want to. Let it all come out.' Like a child she soothed him, remembering how she had gentled Diarmid, slipping a hand under his belt, undoing it, quietly fondling him as they sometimes did to keep the babies hushed, and when he was ready guided him easily into her, comforting, comfortable, while he still sobbed a little. A moment after he was asleep his mouth fallen open and a dribble of saliva seeping onto her shoulder.

'You won't get bored?' he said.

'Bored my darling?'

'With doing the same things again and again? With being happy and making love?'

'That would just be perverse. Besides when I like something I never get tired of it. Sometimes I get a little frightened by how much pleasure you give me. But that's all. I just want it to go on, this closeness. Are you afraid of being happy?'

'No, no. Only not used to it, and yet now I know it it's as necessary as breathing and so I get frightened of its being taken away.'

'Trust me,' she said. 'Believe how much I love you.'

They had spun her around the circle of them as though she was a little wooden top and they held whips to keep her dancing but what she felt was the bruising touch of their hands on her body while they thrust her from one to the other like a brown-paper parcel that must be unwrapped a layer when the music stopped. Except that there was no music now. She had sung at their request while they clapped and cheered, a little frightened that there was so small a difference between cheering and jeering and suddenly aware that the thin line separating them had been smudged out, her voice died with the end of the song and there had been nothing to fill the silence till the flash man called out, 'Tell us the story of your life.'

'I'll not tell you anything man but what I choose to.'

'Come on now,' he said and gave her the first push that carouselled her toward Sadler and on with new impetus from his outstretched hand. Now she was dizzy and panting.

'What is it you want of me? Take anything but don't hurt me.' Kingy stumbled to where she had left the canvas bag and emptied its contents onto the floor. Opening her wallet she scattered green leaves of notes, and coins as freely as pebbles. Then she dragged the rings from her fingers, grazing the knuckles, and flung them down. Clumsily she fumbled with her watchstrap. 'Take it.' One of Sadler's friends held out his hand. 'Will you drink with me men?' She picked up the unopened bottle of whisky.

'Give it here,' said Sadler. She had never liked Sadler.

'We want to know,' said the flash man, 'the story of your life.'

'I've had a wonderful life but it's my own.'

'What is love?' asked the flash man.

'What is love?' she said to Lena. And Lena answered, 'I'll come back and see you.'

'No. Once you go out of that door you'll never come back.' The door closed on her. 'I had pretty hair and teeth,' she said aloud.

'Pretty hair,' echoed Sadler. 'Wash her pretty hair,' and he opened the bottle pouring the cold liquor on her head where it ran quickly through the short grey hair to trickle into her eyes, stinging and blinding them.

'Don't hurt me men. I'm an old woman.'

'Time you was in bed,' said the flash man. 'Send her home.' Desperately she tried to brush the burning liquid from her eyes to see what they were doing. Her coat and the canvas bag were thrust into her hands and she was hustled along the passage to the door. Outside the night air slapped her face and set her stumbling along the road while the door slammed to behind her. 'Lena,' she cried and, 'Why didn't you die then Kingy?' Across the road the common stretched a black bay with the wind muttering among the fringing trees like wavelets on shingle. But she had died; sunk three days motionless as a drowned stone. 'You've had a shock,' the doctor said when the landlady showed her in. 'Don't tell me what it is. I don't want to know. But I'll make it better.'

A cruising police car on the other side of the road made her lift her head to smarten her steps. They mustn't stop her, come close enough to scent the reek of her hair and clothes. 'Walk tall Kingy,' she said. 'Walk tall.' Venus anadyomene, Lena re-entered the dark foam of the sooty common.

'It's because it's so dark and lonely otherwise. I remember what it was like before us and I couldn't bear to go back to it.'

'Do you think I could?'

'Goodnight Percy,' Gliston called, 'and thanks. You did a good job there.'

'Sometimes the old dog's tricks are best,' Percy said and Gliston could tell from his tone that he was pleased though the lights of the highroad gave them both a homogeneous pallor with deep fingermarks of shadow that didn't allow him to make out whether Percy was smiling or not. Did he know what an old stick he was? Perhaps he could hear himself as others heard him but there was nothing he could do about it now, knew no other way to put himself and yet was as amused by his own portentousness as Gliston was by his.

He would walk home. That would take him past the site and he could peer through his knothole and see if he could make out how they were getting on. Autumn was in the air tonight, hanging damp curtains over the streets that held down and intensified the clamour of traffic so that he was glad to leave the high road to turn down toward the river. Below, a blurred and distant nebula must be the fair but which among the galaxy of lit pinpricks he couldn't be sure. Above the battlements of terraced chimneys the city night was rouged on black. Gliston breathed deeply, fogging the hairs in his nostrils with minute drops. Sutherland's, the fish shop, flavoured the air with its aromatic grease. The family had kept it open during the war serving bags of crispies, brittle golden particles, the skimmings, when there was nothing else all through the bombing so no one begrudged them their expansion to a shoal of Happy Kippers. There was still a small queue as he passed and a few late washers in the laundromat with the dazed withdrawn eyes of those submerged in the hour and themselves.

Gliston had knocked out the knothole, even before he knew that they had won, when the site was still littered with wrecks thick as the barnacled hulks his imagination had always cluttered the sea bed with. He had wanted, as he fell asleep at night, to clear them all away, to smooth and tidy the sand for the fishes. The high wooden fence with its sign in weathered lettering, William Smalt, scrap merchant, had drawn him until one night, after a glance all around to make sure he wasn't observed, he had stabbed sharply at his chosen knot with the nail file he always carried as a combined lever and screwdriver and heard the wood pellet drop into the yard behind. Content he had left it that night. It wouldn't do for the mayor to be caught like a peeping Tom. The next time he peered through it was daylight. He had almost expected to meet an eye on the other side looking out but there were only the heaps of battered and rusting metal. 'Favoured corner site,' Gliston had muttered and walked on.

He would put in a compulsory purchase order. It must be cleared and dignified. The wrangling had begun. Now he looked through the hole again. The hulks had been bulldozed away. Could he make out a concrete mixer, its rumbling belly silent, waiting for the morning breakfast of sand and cement, a pile of bricks in the corner, even the outline of a small building though it might only be the workmen's hut?

Yet there was an ache behind the satisfaction. It had been a hard fight, a bitter contest of private and public. Twice Calridge had nearly defeated him. And then he had found the answer in an old map of the borough. He had let Calridge go on, seeming downcast, the fight gone out of him while he haw-hawed and whinnied triumphantly about there being no grounds and the ratepayers being spared the compensation for a private whim of the mayor's. At the end of his speech Calridge was flushed and smiling while the opposition had clapped and cheered. Gliston had lifted his head, a tired yet faithful old watchdog. The opposition had almost felt sorry for him. The voice though still had surprising vigour.

'The property belongs to the borough. The man's a squatter. It won't cost us anything except the price of bricks and mortar.'

136

Five

Percy had suggested a ceremonial opening, fortunately in his private ear or they would never have lived it down. Gliston had answered that it was too much like a funny French film he had seen on television and would make 'guys' of them all.

As it was Calridge had asked: 'And when does his worship intend to cut the pink ribbon?'

'Oh we thought we'd keep it very quiet,' Gliston had answered in his prepared sentence, resisting the impulse to embroider, to add, 'Of course if a few close friends care to drop in for a quick one . . . Otherwise it'll just be the two of us,' knowing that that kind of humour would be dubbed music hall, vulgar in every sense, and lay them open to the opposition's highest flyting.

'Perhaps we should break a bottle of champagne over the er . . . bows?'

And again he had resisted: 'God bless you and all who sail in you.'

The morning had come and gone without recognition. On some official's list it had been added to the column of things to be unlocked and locked again at night. The patch of turf and small beds had been assigned to the rostered care of the borough parks superintendent. Gliston hoped the bench had been delivered. The first day he denied himself the pleasure of a visit.

His knothole had gone when they took away the fence. It was all open now and somehow smaller than he had seen it in imagination or, with one eye closed, through his own private squint. The building itself was in a traditional cottage style: red-brick, slate-roofed, neat and low. Nobody knew but he had insisted on the roses that stuck their green twigs out of the fresh earth and flaunted orange labels of Peace and Perfection, pennants in a stiff breeze. They had wanted to put everlasting shrubs; dark bitter green that would decently shroud the entrances. Gliston remembered the deathly flowering of privet round his childhood front garden and its black poisonous berries, forbidden fruit that had drawn their fingers. 'Let's have a bit of colour. Roses.'

Taking the right-hand path he went in through the open door. It smelt of new mortar still, clean with an aseptic sharpness. Perhaps he was the first one in after all. Soon there would be hatchings in the paintwork, daubs on the cream-washed walls. Never again would it be like this. Inevitably one night the windows would be broken; vandals would desecrate it. He was resigned to that.

He hadn't known that he would do it. There had been no such thought in his mind. Even now as he took the piece of chalk from his pocket the action was quite spontaneous. Carefully, in large print, he capitalled the walls with: *Calridge is a cunt.* Then he went out into the sunshine rubbing forefinger and thumb together, abrading the giveaway dust deep into his skin.

'We have to get out of this bed. Give me a cigarette and some more of that wine and then we must get up.'

After all it had been a great success. With promise of an introduction to one of the ladies-in-waiting D.B. Hackett had been persuaded to stay to the end and had written them a glowing notice. One or two other critics had driven out to inspect them and, as Henry had said, it made one feel quite Off-Broadway, to be noticed in the national press; good for the company's morale and went down well with the councils who supplied the money. The schools had come in block bookings, taking up all the matinees and the slack of the first week. Only the Friday regulars hadn't been pleased and had written in hoping they could soon get back to entertainment: *Someone for Simon* or *Three's Company*.

Christopher had been a bit worried about council reaction but Vera had devised some clever preproduction handouts for officialdom that had made it seem dry school-text stuff with a bit of local color. Hadn't Marlowe been murdered a few miles downstream? It made him almost a native son. The aldermen must have wondered what all the fuss was about and by the time some of them had been curious enough to come and see it was too late for them to stop it so they had opted to accept the national adulation with becoming modesty as though they had been responsible for the whole idea. 'He's a clever lad,' Christopher had mimicked them over his morning egg.

'"Lad" I take it is a relative term,' Henry had flacked the *Times* aggressively. 'I would point out that you had a little assistance with the direction.'

But he was not to be put down. 'You can put your chair back in the attic my dear. Godot awaits.'

'I thought you were God for this week.'

'I've decided to give young Evans a chance to produce. Really I'm quite frayed with all I've been through.'

'And what about the boy?'

'Young Fairhands?'

'Alec,' Henry said reprovingly.

'Fled. A one-rôle player.'

'At least he stayed to the end. He could have walked out on you.'

'"Embrace me, Gaveston,"' said Christopher reminiscently.

'I thought he was rather good.'

'Morality has nothing to do with art.'

'In the part.'

'You're being very heavy this morning.'

'For one who's so frayed you're surprisingly volatile. Perhaps it does you good to be buggered by a red-hot iron every night for a fortnight. I find it unnerving to watch.'

'"Not these ten days have these eyelids closed." I think a day at Brighton to put me on my feet again.' He stretched himself in the enfolding silk of his dressing gown.

'Yes do,' said Henry gathering himself for his exit. 'Who knows what you might pick up there. Whatever it is I'm sure you can find it a fitting rôle.'

He really did feel frayed. It had been a quite shattering experience at the fair when the audience had booed and there had been nothing Christopher could do but get off as quickly as he could without a trap. All night he had fretted that the boy might not turn up and he would have to comb the agencies for some young hopeful from Ghana who spoke English like a seal chewing galoshes but was at least the right colour. It was too late to reorient the whole production. But there he had been in the morning, a little puffy about the eyes and even more withdrawn but with that same controlled sensuality. For the rest of the time Christopher had left the boy alone; he wouldn't jeopardize the production though he wanted him more than ever now that he was beyond reach.

For compensation he had the murder: a violation so ruthless it cauterized desire in his entrails. Christopher had done his homework thoroughly, looking up the exact details of the assassination in Holinshed. As the scene approached he felt his own excitement reaching a new peak until the moment when they flung him face down and he screamed with desire and terror. Every night he drew an echoing gasp from the audience and after the final curtain went home straight to bed.

'How did you sleep?' Henry would inquire curiously in the morning, well aware of his usual much-complained-of insomnia.

'Like a babe unborn,' Christopher would reply brightly. Well all that was over now. For a little art and life had been conflated but they were back to the old repertoire. But first a day at the seaside. He would bring Henry back a stick of rock.

'Kiss me then before we get up.'

'You know what I think about that.'

He did know that she preferred to make nothing of it, to pretend that it wasn't happening, living as she did so much in the moment where the long finger of leaving reached back and stabbed at him. But he needed something to carry away, the taste of her on his mouth, the last image of them together until that image could be quickened again into fact.

They'd done badly by the roses in planting them so late and not well enough heeled in either. The frost would get them if they weren't more careful and protected the roots with a blanket of soil. These official gardeners didn't know the good earth or the lovely creatures that grew out of it, that was the trouble. Either they were book-trained or they were nothing but casual labourers and would flit with the first nip in the air, migrant birds. They were all right for raking the leaves together on the common, golden smouldering barrows she could see between the trees; the young men passing from heap to heap ministering with long rakes and the deliberate tread of those who walk several miles every day. Through the ribs of bare branches in the distance flickered the red blur of buses and the more sombre shadows of cars. She would like to die sitting in the air under a tree, one of those maybe, not cooped up indoors like a hen in a battery. One day after she had maundered about all of a morning like this, with the canvas bag in one hand, her feet in their good walking shoes would carry her over the grass and suddenly just like that give up. But not quite yet. She had had such a life she would have liked to have been Methuselah's sister.

Meanwhile the gardens must be made ready for the winter.

'Good morning Miss Williams,' she said flushing as she always did. 'I am a little early.'

'Oh Miss King you're never too . . . ,' and the voice trailed away as the vague hands tried to pluck the recalcitrant syllables out of the air. 'Do come in.'

'You are most kind. It's time to tidy up.' Kingy hung her mack on the hall stand.

'Yes I suppose so. I do hate to see it looking so bare but you know best.'

'It won't be bare ma'am I assure you. There are still the Michaelmas daisies and a few chrysanthemums. But you wouldn't want the year to look unkempt in its old age. It's like us and we have to keep ourselves combed and clean.'

Miss Williams' own flyaway sandy hair was patted down into a bun but wisps escaped at the temples and blew about her face like striated cirrus. Her hand went up to it now. 'You're right of course.'

Kingy went through the shrouded house into the light of the garden. She had been wrong about the first frost. It had come the night before, laid a white hint that melted with dawn, and gone almost unnoticed. The smell of it touched her nostrils that knew every scent in that garden so well they could detect the least quartertone of change as if, to the perfect ear, the soprano had wavered for an instant. Every season had its appropriate mode; its nature as clear to her as a dominant.

Her own steps matching the young men on the common for steadiness she began to carry forkloads from the compost heap to strategic points. Digging deep pits she planted the remains of the year's growth, the garden waste, where it would rot and nourish the next crop. As the morning crept forward through the sun's arc she worked on, easing the bruised muscles out of their night's cramp. In old age flesh took so much longer to heal. Gradually the face of the garden was made matt and tidy. Miss Williams brought out the ritual cup and stayed to murmur a little over the changes and listen to the suggestions for next year. 'Is that not better?' Kingy asked gesturing. 'Though 'tis a little sad. And now you must excuse me I must away.' She would come another day to prune the roses.

For a moment he lay watching her walk around the end of the bed, delighting in the fall of her flesh, then he swung his feet to the floor and, moving toward her, went down on his knees and kissed her.

'You're all damp,' he said.

'Yes my lover. From you.'

'Can we stop a minute? Wait for me.'

'You be late. Hurry up now.' She knew Stuart was nervous. Quickly he clattered up the short path into the little building in his new black shoes that seemed too large below the thick grey socks. Did she imagine it or was he already growing taller? Alec had given her ten pounds towards the uniform; said he had earned it acting in that play. Now he was gone, had told her the night before that he had got himself a job in the North where he could go on with his studies but earn money too. He was going next morning and had left it to the last minute to say so that she shouldn't try to stop him. He had seemed suddenly much older. She missed him as she stood on the pavement, sharp and hard. He would write. There would be more room now. Stuart could have his bed, and his bike when he'd learned to ride it. It would save on the fares. If he could he would send her some money home.

This first morning she take the child herself. Then he must learn to go alone. 'You do your flies up?' she asked when he came out.

'Somebody had written on the wall,' he said.

'They always writing on the walls. Why they don't buy theyself paper and pencil. Half the time they can't spell the words they write. You pay attention to you spelling.' She didn't mean to nag at Stuart but her own anxiety that all should be well for him on his first day made her over-emphatic. 'Quick now. Here the bus.'

'Can we go on top?' Stuart was halfway up the stairs. Wearily she hoisted herself after him.

The top deck seemed to be entirely devoted to small boys in red-and-grey uniform. Their thin pasty faces peered up at her from under overlarge caps, their ears an ironic comment on the peaks that jutted over the pick noses. Stuart had run ahead down the gangway to the front of the bus and beckoned her forward, turning toward her and patting the seat beside him so that she saw his face too under the peak distanced, and was proud and a little frightened.

The bus lurched and flung her along it into the place very aware that she was the only female, almost the only adult, riding outside apart from two workmen who stared sullenly down into the streets determined to ignore the antics and comments of the grey-and-red tadpoles. When the conductor reached them for their fares she was relieved to see a compatriot face. Stuart had gone very quiet, not at all his usual, questioning self.

It wasn't far to ride. If nothing else had told her, the surge of small fry ('Here thingy I'll bash you you keep shoving') to the head of the stairs was pointer enough to their stop. Please God the bleddy bus don't go on and leave we still up here. But the boys swung down the steps nimble as lemurs and at the bottom she found the conductor with his finger on the bell waiting for them. 'First day?' he nodded.

'That's right.'

The conductor grinned. 'He soon be same like all the rest.' He tinged sharply and the bus shot away, his face still smiling from the platform. Stuart looked up at her, a little pale, the knuckles of one hand clenched darkly around the handle of his small attaché case.

'Do you mind if I go by myself now?'

'Is that what you want? You sure?'

'Yes please.' The other boys were vanishing like a cloud of gnats through the far gates.

'All right then. Don't be late home.' She stood on the curb awaiting a lull in the traffic and purposely not looking back. A dash and she was over. She took her place in the queue. Now she could look. Stuart was at the gate, scarcely distinguishable from the other figures except for the dark neckband between cap and collar.

He brought her shoes and stood them beside her stockinged feet.

'You don't have to wait on me darling.'

'I know. That's why I like doing it. I have no pride with you except the pride of giving you pleasure.'

> Never have something in the faery power
> Of unreflecting love.

The words teased at her, on the tip of her tongue and then slipping away before Hetta could spit them out. Like grape pips. She wouldn't give you a thank you for grapes, never could see why they brought them to people in hospital. Who could be bothered with them when they were ill? Patient indeed. And so she had let the minister know so they wouldn't be silly enough to send her any from the choir. 'Never have purchase . . . ?' No that wasn't it. The quotation had nagged at her all morning since they had brought round the bedpans and taken away the hot-water bottles at seven. She had sat there enthroned, trying to pretend it wasn't happening she hated it so, and to think of something uplifting, and those lines had come to her imperfectly. They were sad like most uplifting things. It should all have been very bright and clean, she did like things and people to be cheerful, because her father had promised her that it would be like her birthday party and then someone, or perhaps a cold draught from a too-open window onto the world outside, had blown out all the candles while her small red mouth was poised and with them had gone the promise.

That 'faery power' could have made up for it of course. But if it had touched her at all it had been so fleeting. And 'unreflecting'? No, Hetta couldn't be at all sure that she had ever been unreflecting. Perhaps if the wild beast had leapt out she might have forgotten the possibility of applause and to watch herself pirouetting in the mirrors of their eyes. Nothing had ever taken hold of her and pushed her back against the wall. Did the black nurses feel any different? Were we just cold-blooded because of our climate or because we'd always had to keep up a front like on Empire Day? Hetta was back in the school hall. Her thoughts wouldn't be tied down this morning. They jumped around the years. Where had she got those lines from? At first she'd thought they were a hymn but she couldn't fit any tune to them or visualize the thirty variously shaped mouths of the ladies of the choir opening and shutting to embody them and she'd decided that it was what they called profane love rather than sacred that they referred to and that was why nothing from the hymnal would bear them.

Had they been sung to that evening piano at home while the young men waited? Somehow she began to be sure that they had stood by themselves. Her husband had been fond of quoting but prose not poetry. Suddenly she saw herself. She was sitting at the very back of the class, the highest of the steps, one leg wound around the iron leg of the desk, the flat smell of school ink very strong under her nose. She had been admiring one of her own flower paintings hung at the front and not listening to the young pupil teacher Miss Gwen who was taking them for English on a warm afternoon. Vaguely she was aware that she had been telling the life story of a poor poet who had died very young. He had been in love with someone called Fanny and the class had tittered because Fanny Towler sat in the third seat from the bottom. Miss Gwen had come over the border to teach them from North Wales and she was quite unlike anyone Hetta had ever met before. Her ruler rapped them to silence. She would read them one of the young poet's poems and she began with a lilt that was more than singing that stopped Hetta's breath and made her palms clammy so that afterward she had had to wipe them surreptitiously on her pinafore because no young lady sweated.

> 'When I have fears that I may cease to be . . . '

Some of the phrases Hetta didn't understand but the words trampled through her.

> 'Huge cloudy symbols of a high romance.'

'Fair creature of an hour' was somehow Miss Gwen herself though Hetta also knew it was love. And now she remembered why that moment in a dull afternoon had been doubly underlined, burned into her memory so that parting the years she still found it there sharply delineated. Miss Gwen had left suddenly and when Hetta had asked her father where and why she had gone he had become very red in the face and retired to his room. It was woman's business and she should ask her mother. She had. Mother said Miss Gwen had been very silly. What had she done? She had thrown herself at the headmaster, a married man, and his head had been turned.

'Is she going to have a baby?' Hetta was amazed at her own daring.

'Shush.'

Out of that far-off afternoon she plucked the word 'relish.' 'Never have relish.' Father had relish with his food. Once she had tasted it and it had burned her tongue, hot and vinegary. Hetta had pulled a face. 'You're too young,' he had laughed, tucking into his plate.

'It's not for young ladies anyway,' her mother had said and she and Meb had giggled without knowing why.

Miss Gwen had given the words relish as she sang them. That was why she was so different. Hetta resolved that she would have relish too. But in Miss Gwen it had been a native indwelling quality. Hetta had to cajole and boost hers with continual attentions. Miss Gwen was vivacious—pert some people called it. She had let herself be carried away as she had carried Hetta away that warm afternoon with her words, as her husband had briefly to the high frozen lake.

Now she stood at the water's edge where she had learned to swim looking out over that channel she had never crossed.

> '—then on the shore
> Of the wide world I stand alone, and think,'

Miss Gwen's voice thrilled to its resolution. Hetta held her breath.

'Till Love and Fame to nothingness do sink.'

Taking either side of the quilt between them they made the bed.
    'I'll just have a last cigarette. Do you want one?'
    'Give me some of yours.'

'There've been quite a few changes you'll notice,' he said as he manoeuvered the wheelchair down the ramp. They had given him permission to take her out for her first airing. Soon it would be crutches, then a stick and then she would walk out, slowly at first, perhaps with an arm to lean on, on her own two legs.
    'It's nice to be out in the real daylight. It's different seeing things through a window. Somehow you can't feel them the same way as when there's nothing between you and them.'
    'Except thin air.'
    She laughed. 'That's right. Nothing but thin air.' She pointed to the low building on the corner. 'That's new.'
    'About time too. We've needed something round here for long enough.' Rowe wheeled her toward the common, at this time of day given up to the unemployed and women exercising themselves and their dogs. As if in mockery of the human world dogs of every degree and shade mounted each other, defecated, swapped greetings, pursued all-absorbing but obscure business, challenged and backed down. Occasionally one took the pedestrian crossing to or from grass or pavement while cars halted and drivers cursed. For a little the chair went along in silence while she stared and drank in. Nurse had said not too long knowing the impact of immmediacy.
    'Dad?'
    'What then?'
    'What happened with you and Mum?'
    Rowe pushed slowly, leaning on the back of the chair so that his weight should help with the work. 'It's hard to say. The war didn't do us any good. And I'm not an easy chap to get on with.'
    'I've always thought you very easy.'
    'Well, that's it you see. Too easy. If you're too easy it can be

very annoying.' Rowe the peacemaker, the conciliator, turned his anxious tortoise head to stare across the sooty grass at his own failure.

'I thought maybe with you both coming to see me . . . '

'We'd get together again? I wondered too. But there's nothing there. Eva needed someone more positive and I always see both sides to everything. I never lose me temper and I never lose me head and that's very hard to live with.'

'Should we be going back?'

'Had enough for a first go?'

'Mustn't overdo it.'

Rowe swung the chair around on its back wheels. That afternoon he must say 'sir' and sit with his hands folded on the other side of the desk while management showed its strength flexing the iron fist in the velvet glove. He was asking for ninepence an hour. He would get fivepence. Behind them the dogs bounded and tussled in the brisk sunlight.

Helping her into her coat, he drew the lapels together in front of her face and kissed her. 'It's all an excuse this chivalry,' he said, 'to get you into my tent.'

The bar was swept clean; glasses were ranked gleaming, ashtrays unsmirched by litter of dog end and cindery-grey froth. It had been cool and quiet in the cellar apart from the noises he made himself with crates and casks. Nothing was asked of him except what he wanted to give. Maura leaned quietly against the bar waiting, the midday edition open in front of her. Tom puffed a little as he climbed the steep steps. He would have to knock off the drink a bit. It had frightened him lately how easily he had fallen into violence, ready for a punch-up like any traditional drunken Paddy. A New Year's resolution would have to be made to ration himself to what he could take and not be led on to compete in the alcoholic stakes like a yearling with someone grading him from in front.

'That Terence!'

'What about him?' Maura turned the smudged page.

'He drinks too much—for his own good and everyone else's.'

'You mean you can't keep up with him. You men, you're all the same. Always having to prove something. Why can't you be easy? Let some be good at one thing and some at another. Aren't you a married man with a business and a family? What has he got to compare with that?'

Tom grunted. Sometimes he wondered which of them was the guv'nor. She could be sharp-tongued when she liked and make you feel knee high to a grasshopper again. 'Have you done with that paper yet? I want to see what's running today.'

Noisily she folded it and slapped it down at him. 'Here comes your friend. He's early today.' And as Terence blocked the daylight from the open door, 'Is it first in and last out with you now?'

'I couldn't keep away from your charms any longer.'

'That'll be the day you need an excuse for a drink.'

'I'll have a Guinness and bitter mixed. Give himself one,' he nodded at Tom, 'and what'll you have my darling?'

'Not for me yet,' Tom said hastily.

'Chicken this morning. You won't let me down?'

'I'll have a gin and tonic since you're paying.' Maura set the black pint in front of him.

'Well, are you coming to Brighton with me this afternoon?' Terence took a deep pull and then wiped the froth from his lips with the back of his hand.

Tom shook his head. 'Not today. The nearest I'll be to seeing them run is on Hooley's little screen.'

'You're like children both of you with your horses.' Maura rang the till contemptuously.

'And don't tell me you don't have a little flutter yourself sometimes.' Terence leaned across the bar toward her.

'It depends what you mean by a flutter as the man said. I prefer more grown-up entertainment.'

'Is that a challenge?'

'Call it how you like.'

From the ringside Tom watched them.

'You come with me then.'

'To Brighton? Like Tom I've better things to do with me time.'

Exasperated Terence banged the bar with the flat of his hand. 'Will you come out with me this evening then?'

'Tomorrow's me evening off.'

'Tomorrow?'

'Ask me tomorrow dinnertime. I'll see how you behave til then.'

Tom turned the handle of the cellar door. There was something he had forgotten to do down there. He couldn't think what it was but once he was in there it would come to him. He closed the door behind him and stood a moment in the dark.

They drew back the curtains from the long windows and looked down into the street.

'Look darling,' he said. 'It's been raining.'

'Raining love.'

The compartment was fugged with smoke and morning breath that would sicken him if he stayed in the rank atmosphere any longer. It made him think of being battened down in the hold of a ship though he had no such memory of his own to draw on. Perhaps it was some story she had told him as a child. He no longer thought of himself as a child. What were they doing now, she and Stuart? Alec looked at his watch. Stuart would be in school and she would be shopping on the way home most likely. Would the house seem even more squalid and hostile to her emptied of them both?

Glancing up quickly he thought he saw the row of eyes opposite flicker away from him. It might have been an illusion but it set him on his feet and propelled him into the corridor pulling the sliding door to behind him. Now they would all think he hadn't a ticket. For a little he leaned on the vibrating bar across the window and watched the countryside kaleidoscope past, field blending into field webbed with hedges, gashed with river or canal. Sometimes there were wooden animals or black houses put down haphazardly but mostly it was surprisingly uninhabited considering the density of the city streets, the fifty million packed into so small a plot. In the early winter the scenes were dullingly similar and monotone grey-green or dun. Alec felt himself painted in the same subdued colours although he knew that to the eyes in the compartment he had glowed exotic as a fish in a tropical tank. He wanted to open the door and say, 'I'm not like that,' but knew that any such action would only underline the misapprehension.

The eyes burned through the glass into his back like sunbeams deflected through a lens. Wherever he moved along the corridor it would be the same yet he let himself be driven along, blown litter in an alley, from window to window, the eyes clicking up at his movement and then down again, until he reached the blank end where the bucking caterpillar hood bridged the space between the carriages. That was the answer: to lock himself in for the rest of the journey. The small white slot showed vacant. A hasty making sure that no one was approaching and he was inside with the little bolt shot behind him. Within the mobile cream upright he was safe. The window onto the flying countryside was rippled opaque. If he put the lid down over the pan covering the funnel down to the blurred gravel track he had the seat he had paid for. There were the admonitory notices to read. He could be scrupulously, spotlessly clean. The floor juddered and threw him about when he stood up but there was no sensation of travelling forward or of anything beyond the box he had shut himself in. Once he thought someone tried the door but he kept very still and imagined them going away down the corridor to the next one. Then the outside faded again and there was only the box. Twice he soaped and rinsed his hands and, like a cat, used the third clean lather to wash his face. To blot it with the paper towel he was forced to look into the mirror, barely recognizing the features that looked back. One eye wept from the soap. He always got suds in one eye. He pulled and patted with the towel until it was soggy and he had to tear out another. With finger and thumb he squeezed out a blackhead from his chin, not because it mattered but because it was there. The eye still wept. His skin ached over the cheekbones, taut with tiredness. Spatterings of pigmentation had slipped into the whites of his eyes. Breathing hard on the mirror he frosted out his face. Then he wrote in the cold mist: 'I am the paper boy,' and sat down again on the lid.

At the door she turned toward him, as she always did, with her hand on the catch. They kissed each other hard and fierce, her tongue flickering out for his to follow it back so that he should be inside her again.

The bench was a good idea. There weren't nearly enough places where you could sit down. They liked to keep people on the move like when he was training at Grantham and everything had to be done at the double in case you should stop to think and wonder what it was all for. He would sit here a bit in the pale sun before he went along to the Sugarloaf. At night they collapsed on their bunks, dead men, all guts drained out of them, sixty pounds of equipment dropped on the floor, old donkeys, beasts of burden. 'It makes a man of you,' someone would quip from along the row of cots.

'Balls!' another would answer.

And then a plaintive Wee Georgie Wood falsetto. 'Please Sar'nt, I left them on that last hedge.'

'Don't come the old soldier with me my lad. You're A1 and up the line tomorrow.'

'But Sar'nt I've got no . . .'

'Well ent you lucky then! What you haven't got you can't lose.'

The voices were very insistent this morning. And suddenly above them all she was saying 'Don't sit there too long you'll catch cold.'

'I want to listen,' he said but inside himself in case the passers-by should think he'd gone a bit doolally. It was a sheltered corner, out of the wind. The sun was quite warm for the time of year. The soil of the flowerbeds would crumble under the hands. After his first laid-down barrage his palms were full of dirt where he'd scrabbled at the trench wall trying to dig himself further in like a crab before the next one could find you. 'Nice and dry here ent it?' someone would say between flashes.

'Heavy old thunderstorm though,' he managed to answer out of his fear-parched mouth as mud and metal rained down after the last clap of shellburst. Oh they were brave and cheerful and when anyone asked you you made nothing of it like all afflictions. But it was monstrous and there was no glory or dignity in it. This morning he was quite sure. Sitting on the bench while the traffic roared past in continuous convoy he found himself clenching and unclenching his fists as if they were again full of earth. Anger and fear for his eighteen-year-old self bubbled in his chest like phlegm. He had been terrified that he would shit himself with fright as so many others did, reduced to a baby or an animal, the eye-rolling horses of the cavalry; a complex of terrors: of the thing itself, of the fear of it, of his own body betraying his fear in the stink of death and defecation, made less than a man.

Why was he so angry this morning as if he was alive? They took you and gave you a tool to dig your own grave and condemned you to live in it for months on end like those religious fanatics who slept in their coffins to remind themselves of the last things. 'In the midst of life we are in death,' the padre used to say as though they were all out for a picnic and needed to be reminded that it might rain. And as if that wasn't lesson enough they buried you alive in a slough for four days. Lice and shit, fatigue and terror, those were the glories of it and the only miracle that you survived.

You had thought it justified as the 'war to end all wars' but that too was mockery, a skeleton in full-dress uniform, the obscenity of a posthumous V.C. Every few years the misery began again. Those who were alive, not zombies like himself, happy as sandboys, children building on the shore would look up to find the sun overcast, the clash of voices, the big stick raised, themselves stampeded into irrevocable attitudes.

As soon as you signed that piece of paper you were committed to a way of death; shot in the back by battle police or blindfolded before a firing squad if you tried to say no. You had assented to your own destruction. This morning he knew. They were to blame, faceless authority, old diehard reaction who knew there was always violence to fall back on, that in the last resort they could raise the old cries that drowned out reason and you would follow deafened and blinded. But you were to blame too, for the soft desire in you to fling yourself into the arms of death because living was fierce and painfully continuous creation, for the ease with which you were codded.

'I know I'm going to get killed,' the boy said from the first. They had sent him home and you had gone on, come through. But there was no difference between either of you and the boy out there strung on the wire. You went home the walking dead that was all. He coughed and shuffled his feet. Would anger choke him at last, a thin old man sitting in the winter sun? He got up and turned up his coat collar. He would cross the road to the Sugarloaf and wash down his bile with a pint. But not quite wash it away. He was almost dead but if anyone asked him he would tell them. 'We should have said no.'

The sunlight made them blink a little. A small wind moved a strand of her hair so that it gleamed a moment and fell back. He paused on the step, wanting to touch the wisp of hair, wanting to delay their descent.

'Is it truly all right, for you?' he asked.

'Oh my dear,' she said, 'it is *so* all right.'

More modern fiction from Methuen

John Arden	Silence Among The Weapons
Stephen Benatar	When I Was Otherwise
Thomas Berger	Reinhart's Women
William Cooper	Scenes From Provincial Life
	Scenes From Metropolitan Life
	Scenes from Married Life
Maureen Duffy	Gor Saga
	Wounds
	Capital
	Londoners
Sally Emerson	Second Sight
	Listeners
Harriett Gilbert	The Riding Mistress
Ronald Harwood	Cesar and Augusta
	The Girl in Melanie Klein
Ursula Holden	Wider Pools
	Sing About It
	Penny Links
Stanley Middleton	Entry Into Jerusalem
Valerie Miner	Winter's Edge
Ntozake Shange	Sassafrass, Cypress and Indigo
J I M Stewart	The Gaudy
	Full Term
Michel Tournier	The Erl-King
	The Four Wise Men
Colin Watson	Coffin Scarcely Used
	One Man's Meat
	Hopjoy Was Here
	The Naked Nuns
	Bump In The Night
	Lonelyheart 4122
Alec Waugh	The Loom of Youth

THE HISTORY OF VINTAGE

The famous American publisher Alfred A. Knopf (1892–1984) founded Vintage Books in the United States in 1954 as a paperback home for the authors published by his company. Vintage was launched in the United Kingdom in 1990 and works independently from the American imprint although both are part of the international publishing group, Random House.

Vintage in the United Kingdom was initially created to publish paperback editions of books bought by the prestigious literary hardback imprints in the Random House Group such as Jonathan Cape, Chatto & Windus, Hutchinson and later William Heinemann, Secker & Warburg and The Harvill Press. There are many Booker and Nobel Prize-winning authors on the Vintage list and the imprint publishes a huge variety of fiction and non-fiction. Over the years Vintage has expanded and the list now includes great authors of the past – who are published under the Vintage Classics imprint – as well as many of the most influential authors of the present. In 2012 Vintage Children's Classics was launched to include the much-loved authors of our youth.

For a full list of the books Vintage publishes,
please visit our website
www.vintage-books.co.uk

For book details and other information about the classic authors we publish, please visit the Vintage Classics website
www.vintage-classics.info

www.vintage-classics.info

Visit www.worldofstories.co.uk for all your
favourite children's classics